**"Hurry home," Julia said.**

"Kiss the kids for me," Evan told her.

Julia nodded. She and Evan were back on solid ground, speaking familiar words, exchanging unspoken promises. She watched the taxi pull out of the driveway, holding herself against the sudden cold.

Knowing there was no way she'd get to sleep again right away, and not wanting to go upstairs for her sweater, she took Evan's from the hall closet and went into the kitchen to make coffee. She found a single peach-colored rose, one of the last of the season from the small rose garden in the front yard, sitting in a kitchen glass. There was a note beside the rose.

*Julia,*
*I haven't told you often enough how much I love you or what you mean to me. You are my world. I haven't left yet and I miss you already.*

*Buy something black and sexy and expensive while I'm gone—something you can wear when I get home....*

Dear Reader,

I've always been intrigued by the idea of a soul mate. Is it really possible that for some people there is only one person in all the world with whom they were meant to be? When a woman finds this man, when she feels this sort of connection, does it mean that if something happens to him she can never love again? What does it feel like to know that kind of love? Can it be a curse as well as a blessing?

As with other thoughts and ideas that have taken hold and refused to go away during my long writing career, this one grew into a story that haunted me. Julia and Evan became a part of my life, talking to me as I grocery-shopped, walking through full-blown scenes when I tried to go to sleep at night. I was thrilled when Harlequin gave me the opportunity to tell their story in this exciting new line—Everlasting Love.

After spending six months writing this story and exploring what it means to find the one person you were meant to be with and then facing the possibility of losing that person, do I still believe there's such a thing as a soul mate? I do. I'm a romantic. Always have been and always will be. Which is why writing romance is such a perfect fit. In my mind there is simply nothing better than a love story.

Well, maybe there's one thing—living that love story yourself. I found my soul mate over thirty years ago. The emotion, the passion, the depth of feeling Julia has for Evan were written from my heart and my experience. It has been a joy to share them with you.

*Georgia*

P.S. I would love to hear your "soul mate" stories. You can e-mail me at jgbockoven@starstream.net.

# *If I'd Never Known Your Love*

Georgia Bockoven

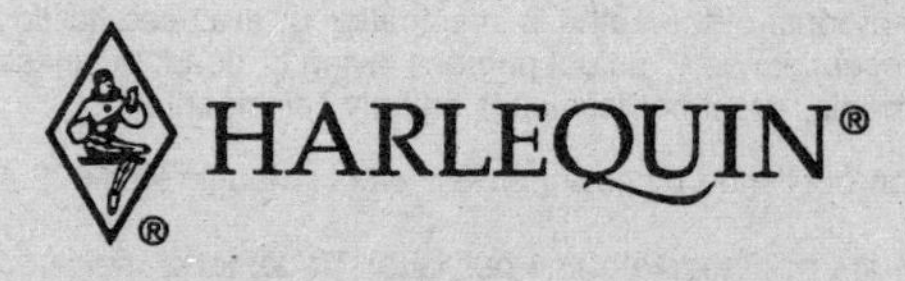


TORONTO • NEW YORK • LONDON
AMSTERDAM • PARIS • SYDNEY • HAMBURG
STOCKHOLM • ATHENS • TOKYO • MILAN • MADRID
PRAGUE • WARSAW • BUDAPEST • AUCKLAND

ISBN-13: 978-0-373-65407-9
ISBN-10: 0-373-65407-3

IF I'D NEVER KNOWN YOUR LOVE



This edition published by arrangement with Harlequin Books S.A.



www.eHarlequin.com

**Printed in U.S.A.**

## ABOUT THE AUTHOR

Georgia Bockoven loves stories with heart and emotional depth, which is why her books have always connected so well with readers. During her career she's collected numerous awards, including a RITA® Award from Romance Writers of America, and has written a shelfful of wonderful books, including *A Marriage of Convenience,* inspired by the dramatic birth of Georgia's first grandchild and made into a CBS movie starring Jane Seymour and James Brolin, as well as *The Beach House,* which launched a whole new subgenre of "deck chair" books. Georgia is married to her personal hero, John, a retired firefighter. She has two sons, two incredible daughters-in-law and four joy-inspiring grandchildren. The household also includes a beautiful Maine coon cat, Josi, who made an appearance in *The Beach House* and has become a bit of a local celebrity.

This one is for Eva Karls—until we meet again

Acknowledgment

As always, a huge thank-you to my docs on call, who answer my questions with endless patience and enthusiasm—John Morelli and Marsha Smith.

# CHAPTER 1

"What are you so deep in thought about?" Evan came up behind Julia as she loaded a cup into the dishwasher. He slipped his arms around her waist, drew her against him and tucked his chin into the hollow of her shoulder.

Julia folded her arms over his and sighed contentedly. "I was just thinking that I should have tried harder to find a way to go with you."

For the past day and a half she'd been telling herself that the elephant sitting on her chest and the panic attack that had driven her from bed in the middle of the night were nothing more than frustration at not being able to accompany Evan on his last-minute business trip to Colombia.

"*Should?*" He chuckled. "Now, what's that all about?"

The queasiness she'd felt as she'd watched Evan pack his suitcase that afternoon—worse than anything she'd experienced during two pregnancies—she'd put off to the shrimp salad she'd had for lunch. She simply refused to acknowledge that the constant, nagging feeling of dread might be anything real, not after all the years of denying the possibility such things existed and that even sane, rational people might be wise to pay attention to them.

She couldn't bring herself to share the depth of her doubts with him. As a child, using maps he'd torn out of books, Evan had escaped the reality of life in a tenement in Detroit by papering the walls of the bedroom he'd shared with his baby brother, and put him to sleep at night with stories of the places they would go someday and the people they would meet.

"I guess I just don't like the idea of you having all that fun without me," she said.

"Hmm…what if I promise to be miserable?"

She laughed. "You would do that for me?"

"Absolutely."

"What a guy."

"And what about you, Mrs. McDonald? Does this

mean you're going to sacrifice all the good times I'll be missing while you paint the upstairs bathroom?"

They had been in their new-to-them, fixer-upper home for less than a month, only their second home since they'd moved to the Sacramento area from Kansas ten years earlier. Was it really all that unusual for her to be feeling a little out of sorts with the stress and excitement? Still…

"Can we be serious for a minute?" She turned to face him.

"I don't think I like the sound of this."

"I want you to promise that you won't leave the city." When he started to answer, she held up her hand to stop him. "Even if one of the people you're going there to meet has a villa somewhere in the country. I want you to promise you won't go."

"Be reasonable, Julia. How could I refuse an invitation to someone's home?"

"Tell the truth—that you weren't able to get the shots you needed before you left. You wouldn't even have had a passport if we hadn't gone to Mexico last year. They know you were a last-minute replacement for Harold. They'll understand."

Evan's boss was still in the hospital recovering from a fall into a hole at a construction site. In addition to three broken ribs, he was bruised all along his left side and sore over his entire body. He breathed like a man easing one last puff into a balloon already overfilled and about to pop. Evan taking Harold's place was not only a huge responsibility, it showed Harold's incredible confidence in Evan's abilities to represent the firm. If they got the contract for the state-of-the-art, five-story shopping center, it would be their first international engineering job and a door opening for future business in South America.

"And please remember not to drink or eat anything from a roadside stand." She added that because she knew Evan would be tempted and also knew just as surely that if only one bug lurked in a gallon of water, it would find him. From the day their daughter, Shelly, had started preschool, it was as if Evan's body had rolled out a welcome mat for every stray bacteria and virus. Neither of the kids had ever come down with something their dad didn't come down with a week later.

"Anything else?"

"Well, now that you mention it, I'd really like it if you stayed at the hotel and didn't go—"

"Whoa, slow down a minute. Who have you been talking to?"

"No one." He plainly didn't believe her. "Okay, I did a couple of searches on the Internet."

"I see." He nodded, fighting a grin and failing. "You want to talk about it?"

She did, for herself, for her own peace of mind, but didn't, for him. If she persisted with her unreasonable fears she was going to ruin something he'd wanted all his life. And to what end? If long-distance paranoia worked, her mother would have a patent on it.

"No," she said. "I'm just—" She shrugged.

"Did you also happen to look up the hotel where I'll be staying?" he asked.

"I did," she said sheepishly.

"And?"

"It looked very nice."

"No-bed-bugs nice?" His eyes sparkled with amusement. "Or four-star nice?"

"Actually, it was the description of the hotel that made me wish I'd worked a little harder to find a way to go with you." It was a lie, but just a small one, and told for the right reason.

He laughed. "And how would you have done that? Two days was hardly enough time to get me ready."

"I don't know," she admitted. "I just should have tried harder."

He planted a kiss on the tip of her nose. "Next time."

"Like that's going to happen. Look what it took to keep Harold from going this time. It's not as if he's suddenly going to learn to delegate just because this trip goes well for you."

"He's getting better," Evan said mysteriously. "I can see all kinds of things opening up for us in the future."

"You did that on purpose."

"Yes, I did."

"You can't possibly think you're going to get away with saying something like that and just leave it hang."

"I'm saving the rest for when I get back."

She actually laughed at that. He'd never been able to keep a secret from her. It was one of the reasons he had to wait until the last minute to buy her birthday and Christmas presents. "Fat chance."

"I'm serious," he insisted despite the grin twitching the corner of his mouth.

Feigning disinterest was the one sure way she knew to get him to talk. "Okay. I guess it will have to wait."

Before he could say anything, there was a shriek and then a thud as something heavy hit the floor directly above them. "What the hell?" Evan said.

A second shriek followed, and thumping on the stairs. "Ee-ee-uu-uu-w-w-w—" Shelly screamed. "It touched me." Racing into the room, she threw herself into Evan's arms.

"This better not be about your brother," he said.

"There's a *mouse* in my room. It ran over my foot. It was so-o-o-o gross, Daddy. Do something. Get it. *Kill* it."

"Think about what you're saying, Shelly. Do you really want me to kill that poor mouse? Just because it scared you?"

She looked up at her father, her chin planted in the middle of his chest, her arms wrapped around his waist. "Yes?"

"And do you honestly believe I'm going to do that?"

"Would you at least think about it? What if it gets in bed with me when I'm sleeping?"

"Okay, and then what should I do to you? You undoubtedly scared it as much as it scared you."

"Oh, Daddy, that's just dumb."

Evan shot Julia a grin. "It appears you'll have to finish grilling me later." He went to the hall closet and glanced inside. "I thought we were going to keep the broom in here."

For the three-and-a-half weeks they'd been in the house it seemed as if they always were looking for something they'd put away in what they were sure were perfect, logical places. "I'm sure I saw it in the garage. I'll check."

Julia finally fell into a restless, troubled sleep at two-thirty that night, an hour before the airport van would be there to pick up Evan and take him to San Francisco for his flight. Evan had insisted she should sleep in, that he could see himself off. She'd insisted just as strongly that she would get up with him.

The soft click of the front door opening woke her. She instantly knew what he'd done and was overcome with a sense of loss. She leaped out of bed and ran after him in her nightgown, flung open the door and shouted, "Wait."

Evan turned and gave her a look of such love and

longing that she would only need to remember this moment for years to come to forgive him anything. He met her in the middle of the walkway, swept her into his arms and held her as if it were the end of their separation instead of the beginning.

"I'm going to miss you," he said. "Every minute of every hour."

She desperately didn't want him to go and couldn't say what he needed to hear, the words that would make leaving her okay.

"Harold is making me a partner," he said.

She gasped. Of all the things she might have guessed, this wasn't even on the distant horizon.

He smiled. "Just what I wanted—to leave you breathless."

"What does that mean?"

"Five percent now, another one percent every year from now on."

"Oh, Evan, that's... That's so...so amazing. I'm stunned." Five percent of a privately owned company like Stephens Engineering was huge. She kissed him. "Congratulations. You're awesome. When did this happen?"

"The same day Harold asked me to take his place on this trip. He said he'd planned on waiting until he came back, but then thought what the hell, might as well give me something to think about while I was gone. I was going to tell you, but then thought it would be more fun when we could go out and celebrate together." He grinned. "And as usual, I couldn't keep a secret from you."

The driver leaned out his window and waved at Evan. "Hey, buddy, I got a schedule."

"I'll tell you all about it when I call you from the hotel."

Ignoring the increasingly impatient driver, Julia stood on her tiptoes and hugged Evan even tighter, kissing him with a thesaurus-full of meaning. "I love you."

"I love you, too." Evan started to leave, then abruptly came back. He held her face between his hands and stared deeply into her eyes. "You are everything to me—always have been, always will be."

His intensity nearly destroyed her shaky resolve to handle his leaving in a sane, rational manner. From somewhere, she found a halfway convincing smile. "Hurry home." She grinned. "We have some big-time celebrating to do."

"Give the kids a kiss for me."

She nodded. She and Evan were back on solid ground, speaking familiar words, exchanging unspoken promises. She watched the van pull out of the driveway, holding herself against the sudden cold. She couldn't tell if Evan was still turned toward her when the van made the corner, but she waved and, in her mind's eye, saw him wave back.

Knowing there was no way she would go to sleep again right away, and not wanting to go upstairs for her robe, Julia took Evan's sweater from the hall closet and went into the kitchen to make coffee. She found a single peach-colored rose, one of the last of the season from the small rose garden in the front yard, sitting in a kitchen glass. A note sat beside the rose.

*Julia,*

*I haven't told you often enough how much I love you or what you mean to me. You are my world. I haven't left yet and I miss you already.*

*Buy something black and sexy and expensive while I'm gone—something you can wear for dinner. No, make that two things black and sexy and expensive—one of them something you'd get arrested in if you wore outside the bedroom. I'll explain when I get home.*

*Love,*
*Evan*

Thinking more about lacy lingerie than dresses, Julia put the note on the refrigerator, then reconsidered and tucked it in her pocket. Shelly was a mature ten-year-old, and Julia wasn't interested in adding to her education. She waited for the coffee to finish brewing. Then, the rose in one hand, her cup in the other, she went into her office to work until it was time to wake the kids for school.

★★★

Julia leaned back in her chair and stared at the newsletter design she'd been working on for the past three hours. The client wanted new and different, but not too new or different; bold, but not garish, with lots of white space, yet not so many pages that it would up the mailing cost. Which meant that the client wanted exactly what everyone else wanted—only different. And, as always, it was a given that the job had to be finished in two days, maybe three—a week at the absolute outside. The three graphic designers who used her on a freelance basis provided a cushion between her and unreasonable clients. She'd become so spoiled working at home that she shuddered at the thought of ever having to go back to work in an office. Thankfully, with Evan's career going as well as it was, especially with the new partnership, she'd never be faced with that decision again.

She glanced out the window at the sound of squabbling finches and saw that the bird feeder was empty. Keeping it filled was Evan's job—his joy, really. Hanging it from the massive live oak that dominated the backyard was one of the first things he'd done when they'd moved in. When he'd spotted the first diner, he let out a whoop that had made her abandon her unpacking and run downstairs to check on him. As a transplanted Kansas farm girl, she found it hard to drum up the same level of enthusiasm over something she'd always taken for granted, but she never let on that seeing the bulbs Evan planted in the fall push through three inches of soil to emerge as flowers in the spring was anything short of a miracle, or that rushing inside to grab a Peterson Field Guide wasn't an immediate response to spotting a new bird or butterfly.

Evan had an insatiable curiosity about everything, and had built a library that contained twice as many research books as fiction titles. He'd passed the trait on to their children, somehow fostering in them the idea that learning was the best kind of game.

Needing a break, she took a scoop of sunflower seeds outside and spotted the mouse that Evan had caught in Shelly's room and released in the backyard. It was sitting on the wooden deck under the feeder, eating seeds the birds had carelessly tossed aside as they sought one more to their liking. With half a tail and a scar down its side from a previous encounter, there was no doubt it was the same mouse. It stopped chewing and stared at her, showing more curiosity than fear. Deciding she posed no immediate threat, it tucked the seed into its cheek and picked up another before climbing the brick retaining wall behind the tree and disappearing under an azalea bush.

In the short time they'd been there, Evan had mentally transformed the backyard, feeling about it the way she felt about the house. He dragged her out there at least once a day to listen to his plans, pointing out which azaleas and camellias he would keep, what he would put in place of the ones he removed and where he would plant the hundreds and hundreds of bulbs that would fill the yard with a rainbow of color each spring.

She mentally added the mouse-spotting to the list of things she would tell Evan when he phoned to let her know that he'd arrived. Nine hours to go. An eternity.

With the exception of a couple of backwoods fishing trips with his buddies, Evan had never been out of phone contact with her for an entire day. He always called from work, sometimes to share something funny or sad, sometimes just to say hi—mostly, he claimed, because hearing her voice brightened his day. Her girlfriends insisted he was a freak of nature, that no normal man married ten years looked at his perfectly ordinary wife as if she were a Victoria's Secret model or lit up like a sparkler whenever she came into a room.

In the beginning she'd assumed that what she and Evan had was simply a slightly altered version of the love all married couples shared. Then she'd stepped into her thirties and saw how few of their friends' marriages were surviving. It scared her. She'd never considered herself unique in anything and wondered if she was simply oblivious to the clues. By the time her own sister, Barbara, had figured out her husband had been unfaithful and had confronted him, he'd not only admitted he'd been seeing someone but told her it was his third affair in their five-year marriage, one of them a woman he'd met on their honeymoon.

Julia tried to picture Evan cheating on her and couldn't. She tried to picture an argument that would tear them apart. Impossible. Finally, she tried to imagine him falling out of love with her or her with him. It was as inconceivable as nonfat chocolate. A really good nonfat chocolate.

Later that night, eight o'clock came and passed, then nine and still no phone call. At ten she put the kids to bed, promising they could call their dad when they got home from school the next day. By eleven she'd traced his flight and learned that it had landed an hour late, but safely.

Figuring they'd been optimistic about how long it would take to get through customs, Julia added another hour to her calculations. That made him an hour late—time that could be accounted for with a few extra minutes to get a cab, more traffic than they'd anticipated at that time of night, a problem with his room, running into an old friend.

The phone would ring any minute.

But it didn't.

She made another pot of coffee, not to stay awake but because it gave her something to do. Fifteen minutes later, she called the hotel. It took several minutes to find someone on the night crew who spoke English. He told her Evan hadn't checked in. She asked to leave a message and then changed her mind. Evan would know she was worried and didn't need a reminder.

Finally, her ability to come up with a reasonable explanation for not hearing from him exhausted, her nerves raw, her mind teetering on panic, she heard the phone ring. "Where have you been?" she said instead of hello. "I've been so worried."

"Julia, it's Harold." He hesitated for agonizingly long seconds. "I'm afraid I have some bad news." Again he paused. "I'm sorry, I tried to think of a way to tell you this that would make it easier, but there just aren't any words. It appears Evan's been kidnapped. The driver hired by Gutierrez Construction to pick him up at the airport said several men with guns waylaid their car and took Evan. Ernesto Gutierrez called the police and then me. I told him I would—well, that I would let you know."

"Kidnapped?" With everything she'd imagined, she hadn't come close to this. "Why Evan? That doesn't make sense." Denial gave her precious moments to escape the horror. There had to be some mistake. He couldn't be one of those blindfolded men and women she'd seen on the evening news, terrified into a shuffling numbness, bruised and bleeding, sitting in front of masked gunmen, pleading for their lives.

"Ernesto said there are a couple of political groups that grab anyone they believe can pay. It's how they finance their armies."

"We don't have any money." *Please, God. Not Evan. Let there be some mistake.*

"But I do. There's no way they could have known Evan had taken my place. They must have thought they were taking me.

"Julia, I can't find the words to express how sorry I am. This is my fault. It should have been me. I swear to you that I will do everything it takes to get Evan home. Ernesto is working on it already. He said he has a friend whose uncle was taken and that he will get in touch with them to find out what we should do. As soon as we hear from the kidnappers, whoever they are, we'll do whatever they ask."

"I have to go there," she said.

"Julia, there isn't anything—"

"I have to be there, Harold."

"Yes, of course. I'll have my assistant make the arrangements first thing in the morning."

That was hours away. "No, it has to be now," she told him. "I can get a flight online and be on my way by morning."

"Let me do this for you. Please. I have a friend who has a charter company. I can get you there faster through him than you can get there commercially."

"All right," she agreed, reluctantly. But she couldn't just wait. She had to do something. She could pack. And call her sister, Barbara, to ask her to stay with Shelly and Jason. Her mother and father had to be told. They would have a hundred questions. Especially her father. He'd never been someone to sit and wait for anything. "You'll phone as soon as you hear something? Anything? From anyone?"

"I promise."

She packed and then called Barbara, waking her, needing her, knowing that she would be there as soon as she could get dressed and drive over.

Barbara arrived in her bathrobe just as Julia finished telling Shelly and Jason what had happened to their father and why she had to go to Colombia. Shelly cried. Jason's eyes grew ever wider as he listened with the rapt attention of a seven-year-old whose only experience with violence was a video game where the good guys always won.

With the aplomb and authority and sensitivity of a kindergarten teacher on the first day of school, something she'd experienced seven times in her teaching career, Barbara took over. She calmed Shelly and corralled her into helping with breakfast, giving her something to do. Julia handled Jason, responding to his endless questions with the same answer—that she didn't know.

After seeing them off on the school bus, her bunny slippers decorated with birch-tree leaves that she'd gathered as she'd hurried across the front lawn, Barbara stood at the bottom of the stairs and shouted up to Julia.

"What can I do now?"

"Call Mom and Dad."

"Okay—but you know they're going to want to talk to you."

Julia came to the bedroom door. "Tell them I'll call when I get to Colombia, when I actually know something. And tell Dad that I know how much he's going to want to be there, too, and that I appreciate it, but—" She paused and took a deep breath. "Damn. I'll call them myself."

"Let me give them the news and then I'll pass the phone to you."

The small kindness tipped Julia over the emotional edge, and she broke down. She flashed to mental images of Evan being wrestled from the car, a gun stuck in his ribs, a blindfold, a racing car, men shouting at him in a language he didn't understand. Had they hit him? Was he bleeding? She hugged herself, her tears punctuated by deep moans.

*Please, please let them realize they've made a mistake and let him go,* she silently cried over and over again, collapsing to the floor. "No-o-o-o-o-o .... Oh, please, please let him go."

Barbara ran up the stairs, forgetting her leaf-encrusted slippers and leaving a trail of yellow in the threadbare green carpet. Crouching to enfold Julia in her arms, she said, "He's going to be all right. Just keep reminding yourself that kidnappers don't take people to hurt them—they do it for the money."

"We don't have any money," she sobbed. "We used every bit of our savings to buy this house. There's no way I could get it sold in time to pay a ransom. Harold said he would help, but—"

"I have some money put away and so do Mom and Dad. We'll find a way, Julia."

Abruptly shaking herself, she moved free of her sister's arms and stood, wiping her eyes with her hands. "I can't do this. Don't let me do this, Barbara. I have to stay strong. What good can I possibly be to Evan if I don't?"

Harold kept his promise and called Julia even when he had nothing to report, innately knowing if she didn't hear from him she would assume the worst. The arrangements were finalized for the flight, and Julia, Harold and a nurse, whom his wife, Mary, had insisted he hire, were on their way to Colombia by noon.

To keep herself sane while Harold slept off the

painkillers he'd needed just to get out of bed to go with her, Julia searched the plane for a magazine, something to distract her if only for an hour or two. She found four on golf, one on fishing and the past six issues of *Sports Illustrated*. She also found a tablet, spiral-bound and blank. With no clear idea what she would say, or why she felt the sudden, compulsive need, she took a pen from her purse and began a letter to Evan.

As she wrote she discovered a peace and connection that were almost mystical. Evan would read what she wrote. She believed that with her heart and her soul. She had to.

*My darling, Evan,*

*I know I've told you this a dozen times in a dozen different ways, but I was a little bit in love with you even before we met. You were all my girlfriends could talk about the whole two weeks I was stuck at home after I broke both my legs jumping out of the hayloft. Of course the guys who came to see me never mentioned you unless I asked. All they wanted to talk about was why the football team that most of them were on was doing so well, and how they were sure they would make the state championship, finally. They thought I cared more than I did because I was a cheerleader and couldn't get to the games.*

*Maybe it was something I heard in my girlfriends' voices, or maybe I noticed how animated they became when they talked about you. Whatever it was, I could hardly wait to get back to school and see you for myself.*

*Looking back, it's easy to understand why you had the effect on them that you did. You were the bad boy from Detroit who showed up one morning walking across the school yard looking like you'd just stepped out of the movie* Grease. *You were Danny Zuko with your long hair and black T-shirt and jeans. Only, unlike John Travolta, you never smiled.*

*You didn't talk, either. Not to anyone. For a group of small-town Kansas farm girls you were the most exciting thing to come into their lives since puberty.*

*Becky Roberts insisted that even the teachers were a little afraid of you. What great gossip you provided for a bunch of kids who'd lived their entire lives in Bickford, Kansas. Oh, Evan, if they'd only known.*

*Of course, hearing all this, I could hardly wait to see you and to win you over with my charm and wit. I was absolutely sure that there was no way you'd be able to resist my cheerleader personality and smile.*

*But you could. And you did. Oh, boy, did you resist me.*

*I spotted you across the quad, sitting on the grass with your back against a tree. You were reading a book, something with a library tag on the spine, and didn't even glance up as I rolled my squeaky wheelchair across the asphalt toward you.*

*"Hi," I said with a calculated, perky enthusiasm as I parked at the edge of the grass.*

*You ignored me.*

*"Hey, you with the book," I tried again.*

*That got through and you looked up, directly into my eyes. I know you meant to shut me up and send me on my way, but for an instant I saw something you never intended for me to see—a longing so deep and sad it stole my breath.*

*That day I learned that love at first sight isn't a*

*lightning bolt. It's like trying to control the drips on a triple-scoop ice-cream cone on a blistering August day. You can lick like crazy, and you just might succeed for an instant or two, but anything beyond that—well, forget it.*

*"You want something?" you asked, still staring at me.*

*I think it was the wheelchair that breeched your defenses, because I'd turned into what had to be a fairly unattractive puddle of swirling vanilla, chocolate and strawberry. Stupidly, I stuck out my hand. "I'm Julia Warren."*

*You glanced at my hand. "You're kidding, right?"*

*"What? People don't shake hands where you come from?"*

*"Not any of the people I know."*

*Even then I realized it was a pretty dumb thing to do. But it was all I could come up with. After all, I'd just fallen in love with the one boy in the entire school my parents would not be happy to find standing at their front door.*

*Thankfully, I was saved by the bell announcing the start of first period. I waited for you to leave, but you were waiting for me. Another awkward moment. I gave in and backed up my wheelchair, hanging on to the right wheel and pushing the left the way I'd been taught to do to get it to turn around. Great in theory, terrible in execution. I don't know if you felt sorry for me or were impatient, but you grabbed the handles and said, "Which way?"*

*I pointed toward the main building. "Thanks."*

*We squeaked into the building and down the worn wooden floor toward Mr. Brolin's biology class. It was funny how all the kids peeked around their lockers to stare at us and how hard they looked to pretend they hadn't when they got caught.*

*I saw Barbara headed toward me and tried to wave her off, but as usual, she was oblivious to anything more subtle than a rock hitting her on the backside. She told you she would take over, that it was her job to get me to class. You told her to be your guest. I watched you walk away, and told Barbara that if she ever chased you off again, I would poison her oatmeal.*

# CHAPTER 2

"I'm sure it's been explained to you that the official policy of the United States will not let me help you negotiate your husband's release, nor can I officially allow you to pay a ransom, Mrs. McDonald. We can, however, provide a list of lawyers and translators without, of course, recommending one over the other."

The man speaking was in his mid-forties, sitting tall in his leather executive chair, commanding, and wearing a navy blazer with traces of pet hair on the left sleeve. While they were only a few hairs, that made him seem human somehow, someone she could reach out to. A removable piece of brass tucked into a wooden sleeve said Paul E. Erickson. She mentally repeated the name several times. After a day filled with dealing with the Colombian authorities who handled kidnap cases and being shuffled from one department to another here at the American Embassy, people's names and faces were blurring. She'd even lost track whether Paul E. Erickson was with American Citizen Services or the ambassador's office. Tomorrow, she would bring paper and take notes. Eventually, Harold would be well enough to make the rounds with her and hopefully pick up what she missed, but not for another week at least, if then.

In varying degrees of helpfulness, everyone she'd talked to that day had told her the same thing. There was nothing she could do until she heard from the kidnappers, and that wouldn't happen for days if not weeks, possibly even months.

She realized that there was no way for any of them to feel the urgency she felt, the panic, the fear that ran so deep it colored every thought with a warning that if she didn't do something right now—regardless of all the learned advice to be patient—it would be too late. All it would take was one more bureaucrat giving her one more verbal pat on the head and she would turn into a screaming lunatic.

"Thank you," Julia said with effort. She stood. "I appreciate your time and will certainly let you know when I hear something." If she'd learned nothing else that day, it was how eager everyone was to be kept informed of the process and progress even while claiming there was nothing any of them could personally do to help. "Do you have a card?"

Her abrupt move to depart took him by surprise, plainly interrupting his oft-repeated speech subtly modified to fit individual crises. He motioned for her to sit back down. "I know that right now it seems we're the enemy, too, and you had expected more from your country, Mrs. McDonald, but there is only so much we can do when it comes to kidnapping. The official policy is rigid—negotiating with kidnappers only encourages more kidnappings—and, frankly, although few will admit it, there isn't one person working here who doesn't feel that policy is foolishly out-of-date.

"Sacrificing a half-dozen American citizens is not going stop these people," he went on. "Kidnapping has become a way of life in Colombia. Go down streets in some of the wealthier areas of the city and you can see men holding machine guns, sitting on top of eight-foot walls lined with barbed wire."

Finally, she'd found someone willing to throw away the script. Julia sat down again, responding to his incredible candor with a pent-up sigh. "Thank you, Mr. Erickson. I may not like what you're saying, but it's something I need to hear."

"There are eight million people living in this city.

Almost all of the country's major corporations have their headquarters here. There is great wealth and abject poverty and compelling opportunity for potential redistribution through ransom. Americans aren't the primary target, however. In total, we don't account for even one percent of the three thousand people who are kidnapped in this country every year. That doesn't give us much leverage. What possible difference can we make by refusing to negotiate, when everyone else does? It's not only shortsighted—it's stupid. And dangerous."

"I'm confused. First you tell me the United States won't let me negotiate, and now you're telling me it's the only way to get Evan back."

He leaned forward, clasping the edge of his desk. "I can't *officially* help you but there are other things that I can and will do. I've already called the FBI, and they're sending someone who has worked on several kidnapping cases in Colombia. He should be here in a couple days."

"How can the FBI become involved when you can't?"

"They've been allowed to operate in foreign countries since the eighties. And because they're independent of the State Department, they don't work under the same restrictions that we do."

"Those other cases…? How did they turn out?"

He reached for a folder with George Black written

on the tab and looked inside. "Of the most recent and ongoing cases, one was resolved in a little over six months, another just short of a year. One captive escaped. And one case is ongoing."

None of the victims had died. This was the first time she'd been given something real to cling to; the first clear promise of hope. While the Colombian authorities had been sympathetic and encouraging, they were also strangely wary, telling her that they were convinced Evan's kidnapping was a mistake, that the real target had been a Colombian oil executive on the same plane who'd left the airport in the same kind of car and with a driver wearing a similar uniform.

"The ongoing case—how long has he been held?"

"Actually, it's a woman. She was taken in the middle of the night from an ecotourist group camping in the jungle in the Chocó province."

"How long?" Julia repeated.

For the first time he appeared uncomfortable. "Three years."

"Oh, my God," she said softly. "All that time." And then, past a sudden lump in her throat, she asked, "How do they know she's still alive?"

"A couple of months ago, the family insisted the kidnappers give them proof-of-life evidence or they would cut off the negotiations. It cost them twenty thousand dollars, but they feel it was worth every dime."

"Those poor people. I can't imagine what it must be like for them." But she was beginning to. They undoubtedly lived every day with the same sick fear that lay in the pit of her stomach.

"There isn't anything easy about this, Mrs. McDonald."

"So, are you saying I should just sit and wait for the FBI agent to get here?"

He gave her an understanding smile. "Basically, yes. But I don't think it's advice you will follow. In the meantime, there are some things you need to hear that are critical for your husband's safe return. One, don't draw attention to yourself or to Evan by going to the media. Make sure your friends and family understand this, too. I know it goes against an instinctive belief—that attention will put pressure on our government and the Colombian government, which will result in quicker action. But all you'll succeed in doing is convincing the kidnappers that Evan is more important than I'm sure he's telling them that he is.

"You'll also give them the idea that the company he works for is in a position to pay a lot of money to get him back."

"They are. His boss has assured me that he will pay whatever it takes." Harold had told her this so many times that she'd come to believe he would sell the company, if necessary, to raise the money.

"But once the idea is planted, it's almost impossible to remove. They will make impossible demands and think you're lying to them when you claim you can't fulfill them." He took a map out and spread it across his desk. "Are you familiar with the factions dividing this country?"

She shook her head. Everything she knew about Colombia she'd learned in the past week, and none of it involved politics.

He pointed to different-colored circles covering the map. "These represent various militant groups that are battling the current government and the territories they control."

Very little land was left unclaimed. Julia looked at him to see if he could possibly be serious. If this was true, Colombia was involved in a massive civil war. "And they all finance themselves through kidnappings?"

"Among other things. Illegal drugs also play a huge financial role. Your husband could be with a group that feels no need to hurry the negotiation, one that's willing and able to hold out forever to get what they want. You have to remember that they aren't on a deadline and don't have the emotional stake in this that you do. They've been at this a long time, Mrs. McDonald. As sick as it sounds, they're professionals. They know what they're doing.

She found the news oddly comforting. Although,

how did professionals make such a stupid mistake and kidnap the wrong man?

"Another thing you must accept is that time is something you're going to have to learn to deal with. If you don't, it could destroy you. I know all you can think of right now is obtaining your husband's freedom as quickly as possible. That's simply not going to happen. At least not on your timeline. There is a process with these things. The kidnappers have to get your husband to a place where they feel safe before they begin negotiating. And even then they may not make contact for weeks. It's a psychological game. They are aware that the longer they make you wait, the more desperate you will feel and the more willing you will be to give them what they want."

She couldn't imagine feeling any more desperate or scared than she did at that moment. She was hanging on by her fingertips and would do anything, pay anything, asked. What kind of men wanted her to suffer weeks, maybe months longer for a few more dollars? And if they would do this to her, what would they do to Evan?

She'd come to Paul Erickson's office with an unfocused, wildly escalating fear. He had grounded her, supplying her answers and hope and direction. "But if Evan isn't the person they thought he was, why don't they just release him?"

"He's American. He works for a large company.

Even if he's not the man they were after, they have to figure he's worth something."

At last someone was giving her information she could deal with. Her strongest coping mechanisms involved knowledge and planning. If she could just focus on these, she would make it. "Who are these people in these circles?"

"The largest are FARC, which is the Revolutionary Armed Forces of Colombia, and ELN, which is the National Liberation Army. Many of the groups operating without set boundaries are small bands of out-of-work drug traffickers who were caught in police crackdowns. They're criminals by nature and unqualified or unwilling to seek legitimate work. Kidnapping becomes their source of income until they can get back into drugs again.

"There are even men who specialize in snatching people off the street to sell to one of the larger, more organized groups like FARC," he added. "They're paid a finder's fee and never have to get involved with the ransom process."

"What would you do if it was your wife or child who had been taken?" Julia said.

"I would hire a private negotiator to work with the FBI. They don't have to play by the rules."

"Where do I find one of these private negotiators?"

For the first time Paul Erickson smiled. "I thought you would never ask." He removed a sheet of paper from his desk and handed it to her. "Of course, if asked, you'll forget where you got this."

She glanced at the paper and then at him. His job, his reputation, his future with the foreign service rested in her hands. "Why are you doing this for me?"

"Because I couldn't sleep at night if I didn't." He smiled. "And I'm a man who enjoys a good night's sleep."

Julia thought about walking the ten blocks back to the hotel but was so shaken by everything Paul Erickson had said that she knew she would see kidnappers lurking in every doorway. She thought about ten-foot walls and barbed wire and machine guns. What a hideous way to live.

But then, Evan hadn't been walking; he'd been in a car on a main road when an SUV had swerved in front of them and another had hit them from behind. Within seconds Evan was gone, the driver left behind, bleeding from a blow to the head. He was the only witness and too terrified to give helpful descriptions of the men or the cars they were driving.

She had the receptionist call a cab and was back at the hotel in five minutes. Exhausted and aware it was an hour past the time she'd promised to call Barbara and her parents, she considered begging off dinner with Harold but changed her mind. She had a lot to tell him and was eager to hear what he'd learned.

The nurse answered the door. Harold was sitting propped up in bed, surrounded by pillows, a phone beside him, his laptop on his thighs, a cup of coffee on the nightstand.

"Come—" He pointed to the chair beside the bed. "Tell me what you found out today and then I'll tell you what my friend at the State Department had to say."

Julia relayed what she'd learned, and ended by digging in her purse and handing him the list of private companies that handled ransom negotiations.

Harold studied the list for several seconds. "Both the firms my friend recommended are on here. Did you get a feel for one over the other?"

Julia shook her head. "I got the impression they're all people Paul had worked with and that he felt we would be in good hands with any of them."

*Dear God. Two days ago she'd been an ordinary woman living an ordinary life, where the biggest decision she'd had to make was whether to pay four dollars a pound for ground sirloin or buy the ground chuck. Could she really be having a conversation with Harold about hiring a hostage negotiator?*

"Then we'll go with whichever one can get here the quickest. Is that agreeable with you?"

"I want you to know that I'll find a way to pay you back. It may take a while, but—"

"Stop right there," Harold said, holding up his hand. "I don't ever want to have to say this again, Julia, so listen carefully. You are not to talk about how much any of this costs or to even think about it. Evan was doing a job for me. He should be home with you right now, and I should be the one those people took. I'm responsible both morally and financially for what happened to him, and I fully intend to see this through, no matter how much it costs." He stared at her. "Is that clear?"

She nodded, afraid to trust her voice.

"Another thing. Evan is on the payroll and will be for however long it takes to get him home again. And, of course, he will also be participating in the profits through his partnership share." He reached for some papers on the nightstand, gasped and grabbed his side. "Damn—I keep forgetting I shouldn't do that."

Julia retrieved the papers and handed them to him.

"I had my assistant get automatic deposit forms from payroll and fax them to me. Figured it would take at least one thing off your mind."

"Thank you." Harold was plainly more prepared for what lay ahead than she was, and she was more grateful than she could tell him.

"Now that that's out of the way, why don't you make those phone calls you were talking about and I'll make dinner arrangements."

"I'm really not hungry."

He smiled gently. "Neither am I. But we both have to keep up our strength for what's ahead."

Betrayed by an overwhelming swell of gratitude, Julia's chin quivered as she fought to hold back tears. "I don't know what to say. How will I ever be able to thank you?"

"This isn't a gift. It's simply what Evan has coming to him." His voice broke. He coughed to clear his throat before going on. "I have the highest regard for—God, that sounds so tight-ass. What I really mean to say is that Evan is special. If I had a son, I would want him to be like Evan in every way."

"I don't know what I would do if—" She couldn't finish.

"We're not going to let anything happen to him," Harold insisted.

*It already has,* she felt like shouting. Instead, she said, "I can't stop thinking about mosquito repellent." She shrugged. "Stupid, huh? But Evan is a magnet for mosquitoes. If he's somewhere in the jungle, I know they're driving him crazy." What she left unsaid was that mosquitoes carried malaria, just one of the diseases Evan hadn't been inoculated against because the trip was supposed to have been a short one and he wasn't going outside the city. Even her ultraconservative doctor had given the okay under those conditions.

"And I keep thinking about him trying to escape

and getting lost." Responding to her stunned look, Harold immediately added, "Now, *that* was stupid. Mary is forever telling me I should have a ten-second delay installed between my head and my mouth. I hate to admit it, but she just may be right."

"It's okay. The same thought has gone through my mind." *More often than she wanted to admit.* A hundred times, she could have added. It was the dancing tip on the flame of fear ignited when she'd first heard Evan had been taken. Amazingly, he could find his way around every large city they'd ever visited, almost instinctively knowing how it was laid out and where things would be. But in a five-acre forest he'd be lost the minute he turned around.

She moved to leave. "What time do you want to go to dinner?"

They set the time and agreed to keep things simple by eating at the hotel restaurant. Julia took the elevator the six flights up to her room, and stepped out of her heels the minute she was inside. She called her sister first. Barbara answered immediately.

"You need to call Dad as soon as you hang up," she said after Julia had filled her in on what she'd learned that day. "He's flying into Bogotá in the morning, and I didn't know where to tell him to find you. I've misplaced the paper you said you left me with all the contact information."

"It's not on the refrigerator?"

"I thought that was the information for Evan, not you."

"I'm staying in the room he'd booked, actually." She looked around at the luxurious suite originally intended for Harold and paid for by Gutierrez Construction. She spotted Evan's suitcase in front of the closet. "The police must have delivered his luggage while I was gone." Her throat tightened and just that quickly she was crying again.

"See? You need Dad there."

"I can barely take care of myself," Julia said. "How am I going to keep him from falling apart? I don't suppose there's any way you could talk him out of coming."

"Not a chance."

"There's nothing he can do here. There's nothing any of us can do until we hear from whoever took Evan. How am I going to make him understand that?"

"He's devastated, Julia. He has to do something, even if it's just being there with you. You know how he feels about Evan. He's as much Dad's son as Fred is."

"How is Mom going to run the farm by herself?"

"She's not. She's insisting on coming here to stay with Shelly and Jason."

"And who's going to—"

"I asked and Dad said it was all taken care of. I have a feeling they talked Fred into coming home for a couple weeks."

"But he just got that teaching job at UCLA." For someone with only two years' experience teaching at the college level, the University of California at Los Angeles was the highest plum on the tree, one Fred had to reach so far to pluck that it was an astonishing achievement when he got the job and was worthy of two days' celebration. Julia groaned. She had no more control over her family than she did the kidnappers.

"Take a deep breath and calm down," Barbara said. "We're your family and this is what families do. Let us help you."

Julia sat down heavily on the bed and leaned forward, her elbows on her knees. "I'm so scared, Barbara," she admitted. "This isn't turning out anything like I'd imagined. I thought we would get here, there would be a ransom note, we'd pay it and then get the hell out. Now we're being told it could be months before we even hear from the kidnappers and then months more negotiating with them."

"What are you going to do? You can't stay there all that time."

"What choice do I have?"

"Oh, Julia—I'm so sorry." Her voice cracked. "I don't know what else to say. How do people keep their sanity going through something like this?"

"It has to be that old cliché, one day at a time."

"One more thing before you hang up. I know it's

the last thing you want to think about right now, but there were several panicked phone messages on the machine today, something about a newsletter you've been working on."

"Damn. I forgot it was due today." Actually, she'd forgotten about it entirely. "What did you tell them?"

"Nothing."

She gave Barbara instructions on how to send the partially finished newsletter by e-mail and where to find the phone numbers for the companies with work still pending. "Tell them I'll get in touch when I'm home again and not to count on me for anything until then."

"What do you want me to tell the kids?"

She tried, but couldn't stop looking at Evan's suitcase, knowing that it was filled with clothes he had packed, a razor he'd used, his aftershave, the notes she'd written and tucked in pockets and shoes. "Tell them I'm fine and that I'll phone them tonight."

"Anything else?"

"There's a peach-colored rose in a glass in my office. Please don't let anything happen to it."

"I'll take care of it right now."

They said goodbye and hung up. Julia went to the window and looked down fifteen stories to the traffic crawling past the hotel. She could have been in any large city anywhere in the world and the scene would have been the same. Too many people trying to get someplace. Fathers eager to be with their families;

mothers going to work every day and wondering if their children were suffering because of it. Some people were happy, some were sick, some were dying. And some, a unique few, were just like her, waiting and hoping and praying for a loved one who had become a commodity.

How did they do it? How did they get up each morning and face another day? How did they go about their lives doing the normal, everyday things that had to be done while they waited? Did they keep their dentist appointments? Enjoy a fine glass of wine? Visit friends? How did they go on with their lives, when she was so consumed with thinking about Evan that at times she had to remind herself to breathe?

She left the window and reached for her lifeline, her connection, her promise—the letter she was writing for Evan.

*Two Days Missing*

*Three weeks to the day after I fell in love with you, I finally managed to get you to actually talk to me. I cornered you after school in Mrs. Winslow's classroom, blocking the only exit with my body and a pair of crutches. It was my first day out of the wheelchair and I'd spent it stumbling around like a one-legged tightrope walker.*

*"Where's Mrs. Winslow?" I asked, as if I cared.*

*You leaned back in a chair that barely fit you and tried to pull off boredom. You weren't just different—mysterious, a little dangerous-looking, blatantly sexy—from the boys I'd known all my life, it was as if you were a different species. And it was pretty obvious you weren't just pretending not to like me. No boy had ever rolled his eyes when he saw me or made a point of purposely heading in the opposite direction when he ran into me in the hall. Well, my brother had, but that didn't count.*

*I assumed at the time that it was the cheerleader thing that turned you off, and there was no way I would let that stop me. I don't think I would have believed the truth, that you were afraid of me and what I might discover, if anyone had been smart enough to figure it out and tell me.*

*"Mrs. Winslow?" I repeated.*

*"She had a phone call. Said she didn't know when she'd be back."*

*"So what are you still doing here?"*

*You ran your fingers through that beautiful long, black hair, sweeping it from your face and letting me see a deep scowl. "And how is that any of your business?"*

*"Oh, cut the crap, Evan. You're not as tough as you want everyone to think you are."*

*You didn't say anything, just slammed your book closed and crossed the room, shooting me a look that told me if I didn't move out of the doorway, you would move me. I didn't. And you did. But when you put your hands under my arms to set me aside, my crutches crashed to the floor. Which meant that you either had to keep holding me or let me fall.*

*"Damn it."*

*I laughed. I couldn't help it. The real surprise was that after a couple of seconds, you laughed, too. The transformation took my breath away. Plainly, there are levels to love at first sight, steps you either take forward or backward once you get past that initial melted-ice-cream feeling. I knew at that moment that I would only be going forward with you.*

*"Now what?" I asked.*

*There was still a trace of the smile when you said, "Now I pick you up and dump you out the window."*

*"Aw, come on, tell me how you really feel." To this day, Evan, I don't know how I got the nerve to say those words.*

*"What do you want from me?"*

*"I want to be your friend." I wanted a lot more, of course, but realized I'd be lucky to get you to acknowledge me the next time we saw each other.*

*"Why?"*

*I grinned. "Because you're the only person I know who doesn't like me."*

*"Don't sell yourself short. I'll bet there are dozens—hundreds, maybe." You took one of my hands and put it on the door frame. "Hang on to this."*

*"I will if you'll drive me home. I missed the bus."*

*You stared at me as if I were speaking a foreign language. "No."*

*"Why not? It's not like it's out of your way." Your aunt lived in a rented house on a piece of property a couple of miles down the road from my parents' farm. "Besides, it's your fault I missed the bus."*

*"Now, how do you figure that?"*

*"I was waiting for you by your car to ask you for a ride and you never showed up. When the bus left, I had no choice but to come looking for you."*

*"You're nuts. You know that, don't you?" He shook his head. "People must tell you all the time."*

*"So does that mean you're going to give me a ride? You wouldn't want a crazy girl on crutches wandering down the road by herself, would you?"*

*For a heartbeat I thought I'd gone too far, been too*

*bold, chased too hard and lost you forever. I was scared and mentally scrambling for an apology that didn't sound as lame as I felt, when you mumbled, "All right."*

*If driving me home meant you'd put a tentative foot in the web I'd spun, my dad managed to haul you in all the way when we arrived. He came out of the barn as we drove up and, instead of lending a hand, stood by and watched while you helped me out of the car. He must have liked what he saw, because once I was upright and balanced, he came across the yard to shake your hand.*

*"Can't tell you how much I appreciate you doing this," he said, taking your measure the entire time. "Getting on and off that bus is a real chore for Julia, what with those crutches and all. Stepping up and giving her a ride till she's on her feet again is a right nice thing for you to do."*

*I almost laughed at my university-educated father's attempt at homespun but would have stuffed a sock in my mouth before I let you know that you'd been had. Plainly, my dad saw something in those few minutes you were helping me out of the car that he felt was worthy of his precious daughter. Or at least of withholding judgment at the bad-boy image you projected. Which was so out of character for him and his usual cranky behavior with the boys I brought home that I couldn't help but wonder if this new strategy wasn't some perverse plan to drive you away.*

*You could have protested, of course, made up some excuse for not being able to give me a ride, but you didn't even try. You looked at my father with a kind of quiet understanding. "What time should I be here in the morning?"*

*"Julia?" Dad asked.*

*"Seven-thirty." For once I managed brevity.*

*You nodded and moved to leave.*

*Dad stuffed his hands in his back pockets and shifted his weight, studying you as you rounded the car. Obviously, he wasn't ready to give me over to you for those "kindly" rides to and from school without getting to know you better, because he said, "If you're not in a hurry I can show you around the place a little. You don't look like someone who's spent a lot of time on a farm."*

*You surprised both of us when you said, "I'd like that." You gave my dad a lopsided grin. "You can tell that just by looking at me, huh?"*

*I now know my dad experienced his own version of love at first sight that day. He had a passion for the land and farming second only to his family. You not only embraced that passion, you absorbed it and made it your own.*

*During dinner that night Dad told us that you were curious about everything, eager to know the why and how and when of whatever he told you, whether it was crop rotation or grain lost to rodents or hail damage. An hour turned into two, and when Mom said supper was on the table, Dad said he tried to talk you into staying, but you begged off. You weren't ready.*

*Or maybe it was simply that you didn't know us well enough yet, that you were terrified of what would happen if you let us in and we discovered everything about you was a lie.*

# CHAPTER 3

Three-and-a-half weeks passed and nothing. Not a word from the kidnappers. Paul Erickson, from the State Department, George Black, from the Federal Bureau of Investigation, and Matt Coatney, from International Security Operations, had used every resource they had to try to find out who had taken Evan and why they were waiting so long to make contact. No one knew anything. Or if they did, they weren't talking.

All three men told Julia not to read anything ominous into the silence, and she heeded their advice most of the time. But when she'd finished her phone calls at night and was alone in her room, with only

Evan's shirt or jacket to wrap around her, his socks on her feet to give her comfort, absorbed by her letter and memories, she didn't do nearly as well as she tried to make everyone think she was doing.

Shelly and Jason couldn't understand the delay, no matter how many times she tried to explain. They wanted her home. Shelly cried almost every night when Julia called. Jason just got harder and harder to talk to.

Barbara and her mother assured her that everything was fine, that the kids were dealing with her absence all right—at least, most of the time—and that Julia should concentrate on what she had to do and they would continue to do everything they could to make sure Shelly and Jason understood why Julia had to stay in Colombia.

Guilt became as familiar as the small mole at the corner of her eye, something she accepted as readily. Someday, somehow, she would find a way to make them understand why she'd seemingly abandoned them to stay in Colombia with their father. She knew how desperately they needed her because she needed them every bit as much. But Evan needed her more. Wherever he was, the one thing he could count on, the one thing she believed that he understood without question, was that she was in Colombia, doing everything she could to bring him home.

Her father had stayed two weeks, leaving with a promise to return as soon as he could make arrangements for someone to take care of the farm. As much as she'd insisted she hadn't wanted him there, she had fallen apart when he'd left. She'd stayed in her room all the next day. When Harold had called to check on her, she'd told him she had cramps—the one sure way she knew to keep him from asking more questions.

She had pulled herself together by the next morning and started working on a plan to get Harold to go home to be with his family for Thanksgiving.

"It's not going to happen, Julia," he'd told her over breakfast. "Mary and I have discussed it, and she agrees with me. My place is here with you and Evan."

"I'm not saying that I think you should *stay* home, Harold. I understand how important it is for you to be here when they finally contact us. But even if we should get a demand while you're gone, you know we're not going to do anything before you get back."

After making them wait this long, Matt and George both insisted it was critical that they wait at least a week before answering the kidnappers, once they did make contact. Intellectually, she understood the process and how dangerous it would be to seem too eager; emotionally, she had miles to go. The dreams that threaded their way through her sleep—the images of Evan beaten and starving, huddled in the corner of a dirt-floor hut or, worse yet, left without any shelter at all—carried into the day, overwhelming her when she least expected it, leaving her shaken and sick to her stomach with fear.

"I'm not sure I'll be able to do that, Julia. I don't understand this game playing. I especially don't understand why we can't just pay them the money and be done with it."

"It's because you don't think like them, Harold," she said patiently, going over old territory. "If we just hand over the money, they'll get the idea that there's a lot more where that came from and they'll up the demand. We have to make them believe they're getting everything they can possibly get or they'll never release Evan." George and Matt had cited case after case where things had gone wrong, and almost always it came down to missteps in the negotiating process.

There were so many small things she never could have known without their expertise, such as using pesos instead of dollars for negotiating, that showing restraint didn't indicate weakness even to the most hardened criminals and that one of the most important aspects of time passing was that it would allow Evan to bond with his kidnappers, which would likely increase his chances of being released unharmed. The more she learned, the more it terrified her to think of what she didn't know.

Harold finished his breakfast and put his napkin beside his plate. "Is your father coming back to spend Thanksgiving with you?"

If she made the lie too big, he would never believe her. "He's trying. But even if can't make it, I've been invited to dinner with Paul Erickson and his wife. So I won't be alone." At least she could see he was considering leaving.

"You know you really need to spend some time at the office, too," she added. "You may have the best people in the business working for you, but they need your guidance once in a while. Especially with both you and Evan gone."

"There really isn't any reason you couldn't fly home for a couple of days, too," he said reluctantly, giving a little. "Shelly and Jason must feel lost without you."

She pushed her plate away, hoping Harold hadn't noticed how little she'd eaten. She had trouble getting food past the constant lump of fear in her throat. When she did, she invariably wound up sick to her stomach.

"I thought about it," she said. Every minute of every day. "This is beyond hard on the kids." She was haunted by the thought her children could wind up with lifelong scars from what they might someday perceive as neglect. "I hear it in their voices every night." Along with the tears that shredded her aching heart. "But I can't leave until we hear something." No matter how she hurt for her children, they were with people who loved and cared for them. Evan had no one.

"What about bringing them here? Don't they get a week off school at Thanksgiving?"

She shook her head emphatically. "I don't want them anywhere near this place. Even the idea terrifies me."

"I knew it was a stupid suggestion the second I made it." He flagged the waiter and gave him his credit card. "I'm afraid I'm not doing very well with this whole business, Julia. I've never felt this helpless. Or this useless. I function best when I have something to do."

"Me, too, Harold." She reached across the table to touch his hand. "It would help us both if you went home for a couple of days."

"What would you do here alone?"

"I'd double up on my Spanish lessons. And Paul's wife, Luanne, has offered to show me around the city. She's convinced I'll find solace visiting the colonial churches. She said there were a couple of pre-Colombian gold exhibits I might like, too." Julia had politely nodded and kept her mouth shut when hearing of all the delights in Bogotá. How anyone could think she'd be interested in playing tourist while waiting to hear whether her husband was alive or dead was beyond her. But then, as she'd been told over and over again, kidnapping was a way of life here. You either found a way to live with it or it destroyed you.

"You're not fooling me, you know."

She shrugged and released his hand. "It was worth a try."

"Why is it so important to you that I leave?"

"It's not that I want you to leave, Harold. It's that I want to stop feeling guilty about keeping you here."

"Ah, I should have guessed." He took his credit card from the waiter and signed the receipt. "I don't agree with you, but I do understand what you're saying. I promise I'll consider it."

Harold flew out the same day that Julia's father flew in. Before he left, he saw her settled into an apartment, a place she could feel more rooted and cook an occasional meal for herself. It also had an extra bedroom for her father. When she met him at the airport, she dropped all pretense that she wasn't ecstatic to see him.

"Any news?" he asked on the taxi ride back to the hotel.

"I can count to a hundred in Spanish."

"You're going to have to learn to count a lot higher than that," Clyde said.

The implication of his words hung heavily between them for several seconds. Then they looked at each other, and in a moment of insanity born out of exhaustion, they started laughing.

Seconds later Julia's desperate laughter dissolved

into tears. She moved into her father's outstretched arms. "I'm so glad you're here, Daddy," she sobbed into his shoulder. "Thank you for not listening to me."

He kissed her forehead. "You're welcome, sweetheart. Before I forget, your mother wanted me to tell you that she sends her love—and some molasses cookies that she got up at two o'clock this morning to bake."

Deciding a change of scenery would be good for the kids, her mom had taken them to the farm for the holiday. "I *hate* molasses cookies," Julia told him.

Clyde chuckled. "I know you do. But somehow your mother got it in her head that they were your favorite."

"They're Evan's favorite," she whispered. "She baked them for him."

"Well, maybe he'll get to eat them. Nothing wrong with hoping for our own little miracle for Thanksgiving."

She put her arm around his waist. "Nope, nothing wrong with that at all."

He pulled a small package out of his coat pocket and handed it to her. "Your mother and I bought you a present. It's one of those gifts that's as much for us as it is for you."

She smiled when she saw what it was—a new cell phone. "I assume there's something special about this one?"

"It's guaranteed to work. As long as you stay in the city, of course."

★★★

There was a small miracle over Thanksgiving, just not the one they'd hoped for. They received word through the local police that one of their undercover operatives had spotted a man who fit Evan's description in a small jungle village somewhere between Bogotá and Tunja. The informant said that Evan had a beard and that his wrists were red from having his hands tied, but that otherwise he seemed healthy. By the time the police had arrived, however, he was no longer there.

The image of Evan was burned into Julia's mind, and was one she would carry with her forever. Appearing unbidden, it was like a hand taking hold of her heart and squeezing. Tears of frustration and fear and longing would tighten her throat and spill from her eyes and she would be lost in a cloud of agony.

As soon as they could, Julia and Clyde pored over maps of the region, noting the average nine-thousand-foot altitude, the amount of rainfall and temperature in this part of the Andes Mountains. Because of the direction the kidnappers had taken, Matt and George both figured it was the ELN, the National Liberation Army, that had taken Evan, and aggressively went after the contacts they had within that organization. The local authorities questioned their own informants and talked to a man who had been released recently from the same region. Nothing.

The kidnappers finally broke their silence in the middle of February. The ransom demand arrived a week to the day after an article about Americans being held hostage overseas appeared in a popular newsmagazine in the United States. It was an in-depth piece about the dangers of traveling to certain countries and included a lengthy sidebar with pictures of several hostages, including Evan. The information and photograph had been supplied by Harold's assistant, one of the few people they'd forgotten to tell not to give interviews. Undoubtedly believing she was helping, she'd told the reporter how important Evan was to Stephens Engineering, adding the unpublicized fact that he'd recently been made a partner.

George Black called her on Valentine's Day, her cell phone ringing in the middle of her Spanish class at the Embassy. "Julia, it's George. Do you have a minute?"

She got up and left the classroom. "I always have a minute for my favorite FBI guy." She moved farther down the hallway, where the reception was better. "What's up?"

"We've heard from the people who have Evan."

Her knees went weak. She put her hand against the wall for support. "And?"

"They're asking for ten million."

She did a quick calculation. "What is that? About

forty-five hundred American?" That was not only doable, she should have at least that much in her checking account. If not, she could get a cash advance on her credit card. Had she ever learned how, she would have done a cartwheel right there in the hallway.

"Not pesos, Julia," George said. *"Dollars."*

Five seconds of joy. Was that all she was given after four months of agony? It wasn't fair. She fought to keep the fury and frustration from her voice. "I don't understand. Why so much? We can't possibly pay it. What in the world would make them think we could?"

"Obviously, someone got hold of the article and figured if Evan was a partner in Stephens Engineering he must be worth a lot of money. I don't know...." For a brief, rare instant, he sounded discouraged. "Maybe this is what they've been waiting for all along."

"Do we know who has him? Is it the ELN?"

"They didn't identify themselves. My guess is they decided that for someone this valuable and with this amount of money involved it's more important to get paid than take credit."

She squeezed her eyes closed to block the inevitable tears and tried to concentrate on the fact that at last they had what they'd been waiting for—contact. "Now what?"

"We begin the negotiating process."

"How far will they come down?"

"I have no idea," he admitted.

"We can't pay ten million," she repeated. "That kind of cash outlay would cripple the company." Pain radiated through her like a sprung roll of barbed wire.

"I'm going to tell you something you already know but might need reminding. Every time you get frustrated with the process think about this."

She nodded, even knowing he couldn't see her.

"Negotiation is like creating a statue out of a block of marble. It's imperative to understand the stone before you strike a blow. Once something is removed, it can't be replaced. If we make a misstep with these people, we can't go back and start over."

"What do you want me to do?"

"As soon as we give them an answer, I want you to go home and see your kids and not return for a couple of weeks. There's no way we're going to hear from them again sooner than that."

"When will we answer them?"

"We're still working on that."

For the first time she felt an unbearable sense of hopelessness. She desperately wished she hadn't talked her father into leaving again. "I understand."

"I know you do," he said softly. "And I know that understanding doesn't make it any easier. Just keep telling yourself that this is a good thing. We've finally heard from them."

*Four Months Missing*

*For seventeen years I'd lived in a cocoon, sheltered by parents who loved me and believed without question that I was special, and a brother and sister who didn't just tolerate me but actually liked me. At least most of the time.*

*Which meant I wasn't prepared when you told me the truth about yourself and broke my heart. I had no point of reference to understand that kind of pain. I knew without hesitation that my mother would lay down her life for her children. I couldn't conceive her being so self-absorbed that one of us would die as a result of her carelessness. It was impossible to imagine her turning to heroin to ease her pain or that she could pass out and leave something so dangerous within the reach of a four-year-old.*

*When your mother killed herself out of guilt, she couldn't have understood what it would do to you, how finding her sitting in a bathtub full of blood would be the way you would remember her forever, and how starkly alone you would be without her and your brother. But then, maybe she thought she was doing you a favor, and that you were better off without her. Maybe it was the only way left for her to tell you that she loved you. All I know for sure is that you wouldn't have moved to Kansas if she hadn't died, and we wouldn't have found each other. When I get angry with her for doing what she did to you and the way she did it, I remind myself of that.*

*Did I ever tell you that my father had only known you a couple of months and wanted to adopt you? Somehow he found out your aunt would only let you stay with her as long as the state paid for your keep. I threw a holy fit when I heard him discussing it with my mother. Of course I couldn't just come out and say that I was in love with you, that I put myself to sleep at night planning our wedding, and how awkward it would be to explain to everyone that I was marrying my brother. My mom must have figured it out and clued in my dad, because he never mentioned it again. He did, however, spend a lot of time with us that we could have been spending alone.*

*Mrs. Winslow got involved when she discovered you were two years behind where you should have been as a high-school senior. She volunteered to help you catch up, promising to keep your secret as long as you came to her classroom after school every day and made progress. Dad and I pretty much ruined that for you when he made you my chauffeur, leaving you caught between a hunger to learn and a need to belong somewhere.*

*I had no idea what I'd done until Mrs. Winslow drew me aside one day and told me she was going to have to go to the principal if you didn't start showing up for her after-school sessions. Of course she assumed*

*I knew what she was talking about, and I was smart enough to listen to that little voice in the back of my head telling me to play along.*

*That night on the way home I confronted you. I'd convinced myself that we were friends by then and was angry, and more than a little hurt, that you hadn't said anything. You just let me go on messing things up for you even after I'd reached the point I could do a pirouette on my crutches and no more needed help getting on and off the bus than the flies that came on board every day when we dropped Hazel off near the fertilizer plant. As hard as it was to admit, I secretly thought you were a lot more worried about losing your growing friendship with my dad than you were with losing my company.*

*You didn't say anything for a couple of miles, then pulled off the road at Branford Creek. We bumped along the rutted dirt road in silence until you found an opening where you could park beside the creek.*

*We'd had a dry summer, and the cottonwood leaves had shriveled and dropped prematurely, leaving the trees looking sad and desolate. I saw the same emptiness in your eyes when you turned to me. Until that afternoon I'd lived a white-bread-and-mayonnaise life, never doubting that I was loved, never faced with a decision harder than which dress to buy for the prom.*

*Then you told me about your mother and little brother, and I was irrevocably thrust from the innocent, sheltered world my parents had created for me into a world where terrible things happened to good people. I cried and you frowned, breaking my heart all over again. You couldn't understand how I could shed tears over someone I'd never met or how I could grieve for someone I'd known less than a month.*

*"There's more," you said reluctantly after I'd finally stopped crying and dried my tears.*

*"How could there be?" I said, tears instantly welling in my eyes again.*

*"This is different. I really don't care who knows about my mother and brother. If someone thinks I'm nothing but a piece of shit because of them, that's their problem. But this other thing is my problem. You can't tell anyone, Julia."*

*"I won't."*

*"You have to promise."*

*I eagerly nodded. "I do."*

*"Are you sure?"*

*I crossed my heart and put my finger on the tip of my nose so that my eyes were crossed, too, then grinned. "What more could you ask?"*

*"This is serious, Julia. If you tell anyone and they tell the wrong person, I'll be arrested and spend the next ten years of my life in prison."*

# CHAPTER 4

*Five Years Later*

Julia McDonald stared at the black suit she'd packed only moments earlier and wondered if it was too somber. It might be better to go with something lighter, the buttercup-yellow or maybe even the sea-foam green, a color that made her look more confident than she felt. She stared at the closet, contemplating her choices. Before Evan was kidnapped, she hadn't owned a single suit; now she owned ten.

"Still can't decide, huh?" Shelly said between bites of a banana, uncharacteristically early for school.

"What do you think of this one?" Julia asked, glancing at her daughter in the mirror, noting she'd changed from the sweater she'd had on earlier to the sweatshirt with UCLA written across the front in six-inch-high letters. Her uncle Fred, the UCLA professor, had sent it for her fifteenth birthday the previous week, innocently insisting he wasn't recruiting, just advertising.

Shelly studied her mother's reflection. "It's okay, I guess."

"It can't just be okay. It has to be perfect."

"Then go with the red one."

"I can't wear red for this."

"Why not?"

"It's not serious enough."

"How can it not be serious when it's in the Colombian flag?"

"It just seems too happy."

"Why shouldn't you be happy? Isn't the whole purpose of this thing to convince the Colombian ambassador we think Dad is still alive?"

"We don't *think* he's alive," she snapped. "And the purpose is to get them to start actively looking for him again."

"I thought the *purpose* was to bring Dad home," Shelly snapped back.

They had been on the verge of an undefined argument all week, Shelly moody, Julia preoccupied, her patience threadbare. "What is your problem? You've been like this for days."

"Sorry," she said without real regret. "I'll get over it. I always do, don't I?"

Julia shut the closet door. She had plenty of time to pack after Shelly left for school. "I'm sorry, too."

Sorry for so many things that she'd stopped counting. A third of Shelly's childhood had been consumed in the frustrating, heartbreaking struggle to bring her father home. Julia had missed holidays and birthdays, chasing promises that she knew better than to believe but couldn't ignore. "This meeting has me rattled." She offered a smile to go with the apology. "You'd think I'd be used to them by now."

"Yeah, me, too." She folded the banana skin back onto itself and stuffed it into an empty water glass on the nightstand next to the peach-colored rose Barbara had had freeze-dried and preserved for Julia. After five years it had faded and was showing wear, but had not lost one petal. It was the last thing Julia looked at each night, the memory that put her to sleep.

Shelly picked up the small, framed photograph beside the lamp, the last one taken of them as a family. They were in the backyard, stiffly posed, waiting for the remote to take their picture. Seconds later they had burst out laughing, Evan grabbing Shelly and Jason around their waists and swinging them in a circle.

"I look so different." She sat on the corner of the bed. "I'll bet Dad won't even recognize me when he sees me again."

Feeling a breath-stealing wave of love that Shelly had made the effort to say *when* and not *if,* Julia sat next to her and put her arm across her daughter's shoulders for a quick hug. In five years Shelly had gone from an awkward ten-year-old with twin pony-tails and Chiclets teeth to a young woman who turned the heads of young boys and men old enough to know better.

"He'll be surprised," Julia said. "I'm sure it's something he thinks about all the time, but I'm just as sure he has it all wrong."

"Why?"

"Your father's never had a very good imagination. He's a born engineer, practical and methodical." She and Evan were the opposites that formed the perfect whole. She was the kite, Evan the tail, both made to function best with the other.

"I don't remember what Dad's like…not really. I have all the pictures in my head that I'm supposed to have, but it's like they're not connected to a real person anymore."

"Sometimes it feels a little like that for me, too." It was a lie, but one Evan would understand. She remembered everything about him, from the way he felt spooned against her in the morning to the way he walked into a crowded room and searched faces until he found her. And then came his smile—in recognition, in discovery, in love. She could easily imagine herself stepping into his arms and know exactly how it would feel, where her head would touch his chin, how he would smell.

Shelly stared at the photograph. "Jason hasn't changed as much as I have."

"Not yet. But there are some big changes coming."

"Did you know he thinks he's getting a beard? I caught him looking in the mirror the other day and he tried to convince me there was something growing on his chin. It's so dumb—like having hair on your face makes you special."

"At twelve it does." She smiled. "At thirty it's a pain in the butt."

"Do you ever wonder what Dad's like now?"

Julia started to answer, but Shelly cut her off. "What if he's nothing like he used to be? What if he actually likes Colombia and doesn't want to leave? Would we have to move there?"

"No one can go through what your father's gone through and not be changed by it. But I can guarantee he's not going to ask us to move."

"I'm so tired of this. I just want it to be over." Shelly put the photograph back on the nightstand and stood.

"I know how hard this is on you and Jason."

"No, you don't," she fired back. "You don't have a clue what it's like for us. You think you do, but you don't."

"Then tell me."

"I can't. It would hurt your feelings."

"I can take it."

Shelly hesitated. Her lower lip trembled with the effort to hold back tears. "Sometimes I think it would be better if they had just shot Daddy instead of kidnapping him. At least then we'd know what happened and we wouldn't have to live like this."

Julia was torn between outrage and grief. "You don't mean that."

"I just want us to be like we used to be." A sob caught in her throat.

Julia took Shelly in her arms. "What we used to be is gone," she said softly. "It's a memory, another life." She leaned back to engage Shelly's eyes. "Now, you want to tell me what brought this on?"

Shelly dipped her head. "You said you'd be here. You promised. Why do I always have to be second? Why couldn't I be first just this once?"

When she'd told Shelly she would be there for her first real pick-up-the-phone-and-ask date she'd meant every word. Nothing would get in the way. She tucked an ebony-colored strand of hair behind Shelly's ear. "I thought you were okay with my leaving."

"You said I could count on you. You *promised*."

"I know. I'm sorry." There was nothing else she could say, nothing Shelly hadn't heard a hundred times before.

Shelly closed her eyes, squeezing out a lone, last tear. She sat there for several agonizingly long seconds before she took a deep breath and said, "And I'm sorry for what I said about Dad. I didn't mean it."

"We need to talk about this some more. Maybe when—"

*"Hey, bat breath,"* Jason shouted from the bottom of the stairs. "Patty just drove that piece of junk of hers into the driveway." The words were laced with envy. It was everything Jason could do not to salivate when he saw Patty's car, a midnight-blue 1965 Mustang with orange and yellow flames painted across the hood and front fenders courtesy of a grandfather whose all-time favorite movie was *American Graffiti*.

Shelly untucked the strand of hair from behind her ear. "Will you still be here when I get home?"

Julia shook her head. "Remember—I told you my plane leaves at two."

"I guess I'll see you when you get back, then."

"I'll call." She always did, at least once a day. "I'm going to want you to tell me all about your date, so don't go to bed until you hear from me."

Shelly nodded and left, bounding down the stairs. She yelled from the front door, "Love you, Mom."

"I love you, too," Julia called back.

Julia gathered the banana peel and glass from the nightstand before she went downstairs to look for Jason. She found him standing at the living-room window, peeking through the curtain. "Piece of junk?" she chided. "I hope you didn't say that to Patty."

"You think I'm crazy? She'd make me and Shawn walk to baseball practice."

"Speaking of walking, shouldn't you be leaving?"

"Shawn's mom is picking me up. She switched days off, so she's driving us on Mondays and Fridays now."

"You already told me that, didn't you?"

"A couple of days ago."

"Sorry, I forgot."

He patted her shoulder as he passed. "Yeah, I know. That's what happens when you get old, Mom."

Julia ignored the taunt. "Take your key in case you get home before Aunt Barbara gets here. She said she had a parent-teacher conference that could run late."

He stopped and turned to look at her. "Why is Aunt Barbara going to be here?"

"Washington?" she prompted. "My meeting with the ambassador?"

"I thought that was next week."

"That's what happens when you're twelve and don't pay attention."

He groaned. "I told Tom he could stay over tomorrow night. His mom's having some guy for dinner and he doesn't want to be there."

Tom was Jason's best friend, their house his refuge for the past year while his parents went through a trial separation that had turned into a messy divorce. "I'll call Aunt Barbara before I leave, but you'll have to check with her when you come home in case she had something else planned."

"I told him you'd drop us off at the mall Saturday. Could you tell her that, too?"

"Remind me—when did I start letting you hang out at the mall?"

He grinned. "Can't blame a guy for trying."

"Get your stuff. I just heard Shawn's mother pull into the driveway."

He glanced at the clock on the mantel. "It can't be her. She's never early."

Julia went to the side window beside the door. "You're right. It's Aunt Barbara."

Her thick, naturally curly hair drawn back in a ponytail, wearing a corduroy jumper with enormous patch pockets, a knit turtleneck and tennis shoes, Barbara looked closer to sixteen than thirty-five. Short, like their mother, she had to stretch to make five foot two—an asset for a kindergarten teacher but a major frustration for a woman who loved long skirts and tall boots.

"Shouldn't you be at work?" Julia said, opening the door as Barbara came up the walk.

"I wanted to give you something. For luck." She

came inside. Noticing Jason, she said, "Hey, kiddo, what are you still doing here?"

"Shawn's mother is picking me up." He glanced at Julia. "Don't forget to ask about Tom."

"What about Tom?" Barbara asked

"I told him he could spend the night Saturday," Jason supplied. "But Mom said I had to check with you first."

"It's okay with me. I like Tom."

"Thanks." He gave Barbara a quick hug and disappeared down the hallway.

"Don't forget your key," Julia reminded him.

"I won't…I'm not the one getting old," he shouted back.

Barbara smiled and cocked an eyebrow at her sister. "What's that all about?"

"He's trying to convince me that I'm becoming senile." She started to close the door and saw Shawn's mother pulling into the driveway. "Jason, they're here."

"I'm coming." Seconds later Jason bounded down the hallway, made a leap to touch the ceiling, smiled in satisfaction at his success and raced out the door. He called over his shoulder, "Bye, Aunt Barbara. Love you, Mom."

"Goodbye, Jason," Barbara said.

"I love you, too," Julia replied, meaning every word. After Evan's kidnapping she'd never said goodbye to her children without telling them that she loved them. Now they were the ones who told her first.

Barbara put her arm around Julia's waist. "Ah, the pitter-patter of little feet."

"It's yours to share anytime. You don't have to wait to be asked." Julia waited for the car to leave, waved, then closed the door. "Now, what did you bring me?"

Digging deep into her pocket, Barbara took out a small envelope. "Remember Mom's four-leaf clover?"

"The one she had at the back door?" Encased in plastic and thumb-tacked to the wall above the light switch, it had hung there as long as Julia could remember.

"I asked for it when they remodeled the kitchen last summer. I didn't believe she'd actually part with it, but then Dad told her it might help me find a man and she practically insisted I take it. You would crack up at the ways she's found to ask if I've corralled anyone yet. Honest to God, I think she'd be willing to drop her standards to eating and breathing she's so desperate for me to get married again. I called her yesterday and told her I was going to give it to you, and she said—"

"That it was a sign and that Evan—"

"Would be home by Valentine's Day. Just know that when he's home, you're to give the thing back to me."

"Three weeks, huh? I wish you would have thought about this five years ago." For the first two years after Evan was taken, her mother had begun every conversation with the latest positive sign she'd seen that let her know that Evan would be home soon—things as wildly varied as discovering a pebble in a bag of split peas to the number of blue cars they passed on the way to church on Sunday. Then she'd simply stopped. Julia had never asked why but had a feeling her father had something to do with it.

"Well, from her lips to God's ears," Julia said. She reached for the envelope and was startled to see her hand shaking, not just a little, the way it did when she was on a caffeine high, but a lot. She stared at her trembling fingers for several seconds, then brought her other hand up and saw that it was shaking, too.

"Is this something new?" Barbara asked.

"I don't know. I think so. At least, I've never noticed it before."

"Is it the meeting?"

Denial was on the tip of her tongue, when she felt a swell of tears tighten her throat and admitted, "I'm so tired, Barbara. Just getting someone to call me back anymore takes weeks and weeks. The ambassador is only seeing me tomorrow as a favor to his cousin Gina Michaels, the new FBI agent assigned to the case. Evan is yesterday's news and I've run out of ways to make people who can do something about it want to try. I don't know what else to do."

"I'm such an idiot. I should have realized." Barbara put her arms around her sister. "What time is Harold picking you up?"

Wary of the abrupt change in the conversation, Julia answered slowly. "Twelve-thirty."

"What do you have planned between now and then?"

"What's your point?"

"You shouldn't be alone. You're going to drive yourself crazy thinking about this."

"I'm alone every day."

"Today is different." She took Julia's hand. "Come on—let me do this for you."

"I'm okay. Really." She managed to summon a confident smile. "Now, get out of here. There's a classroom full of five-year-olds who need you more than I do."

"Let me do this for you," she persisted.

"Save it for later. When I get back."

"Oh, Julia...I don't know what to say. I'm just so, so sorry."

"Yeah, me, too." She forced a smile.

Barbara glanced at her watch. She sighed in defeat. "Any last-minute instructions?"

"None that I've thought of. All the phone numbers and flight times are on the fridge, as usual." She walked Barbara to the door. "Oh, there is one thing. Shelly is upset that I'm not going to be here for her date with John on Saturday, so be prepared."

"I'll have some cocoa ready when she comes home, in case she wants to talk. And if she doesn't—" She shot her sister a wicked grin. "I'll make her life a living hell until she does."

Julia felt a sudden, unreasoning stab of jealousy. She should be the one Shelly talked to. A first date only happened once. The excitement, the joy, the enthusiasm would be watered down or lost in the retelling.

"Are you sure you're okay?" Barbara asked.

The phone rang. "Stop worrying about me." Julia gave Barbara a quick hug. "I'll call as soon as I get to the hotel." She made a dash for the kitchen and grabbed the phone on the fourth ring. "Hello." She waited for a response. Nothing. She tried again. "Hello?" This time static cut the silence, loud, with a hint of unrecognizable speech. "Is someone there?" The static ended. The line hummed.

Julia listened for several more seconds before she replaced the receiver. As she did, an odd, unsettling feeling settled over her. She shoved her hand into her pocket to retrieve the laminated four-leaf clover.

Barbara had the right idea. Julia could use something to believe in, but she'd need more than an aberrant piece of vegetation.

*Four Months and One Week Missing*

*I wasn't as much upset as frightened when you told me you'd done something so bad that you could go to prison. By then I was so in love I would have done anything to keep you safe, including running away with you if you'd asked.*

*"What did you do?" I was torn between wanting to know because I wanted to know everything about you, and not wanting to know because I was scared it would change things between us. But it didn't matter. You felt you had to tell me.*

*"I missed a lot of school when my brother was born. My mom managed to stay clean while she was carrying Shawn, but a couple of weeks after she got him home she was mainlining again. If she'd scored the night before, she would still be high when I left for school in the morning. Half the time she would pass out and forget all about Shawn. I'd come home and find him in a diaper so full that shit was leaking out the sides. He'd be screaming his head off because he hadn't been fed all day."*

*"What about Shawn's dad?"*

*You stopped looking at me then and stared out the window. You must have realized you were talking to someone who had no reference to understand the life you'd led.*

*"My mother was a prostitute, Julia. That's how*

*she got the money to pay for her drugs. If someone promised her a brick, she couldn't have picked Shawn's father out of a lineup."*

*"I don't know what a brick is."*

*You sighed. "Fifty bags of heroine."*

*"Oh...."*

*"I shouldn't be telling you this."*

*"Probably not," I said. "But you might as well finish or I'm going to imagine something a whole lot worse than it is."*

*You let out a disparaging laugh. "Not likely. I'm years behind where I should be in school, but that's not what matters. As soon as I turn eighteen I'm on my own. There's no way I can stay in school and get a job that makes enough money to support myself—not without a high-school diploma. I'd be like a dog trying to catch its tail."*

*"I don't understand what this has to do with—"*

*"Give me a minute."You grabbed the steering wheel in a white-knuckle grasp. "I thought if I could get rid of the transcripts from my old school, I could show up here and convince everyone I was in the grade I should be in. I knew I'd have to do some catching up but figured if I handled it right, everyone would just think I was slow and had come from a bad school. I didn't care if I graduated last in the class. Nothing mattered but getting out of school and then out of here."*

*"And you were afraid if you made friends, someone would find out. So you did this big tough-guy act and drove everyone away."*

*"Pretty much."*

*"Except me."*

*"You have to admit I tried."*

*I put my hand on your arm, but you shrugged me off.*

*"There's more," you said.*

*"There isn't anything you could tell me that would make a difference."*

*"Don't be so sure." You faced me again. "How would you feel if you knew I was responsible for burning down my old school?"*

*I didn't say anything. You told me later that you thought it was because I was waiting for you to finish, but it was because I was too stunned. All my life I'd operated on the premise that there wasn't anything I couldn't fix or make better. This was the first time I'd been hit with something that I couldn't make go away and it was almost impossible to accept. "What happened?" I finally managed to ask.*

*"I tried to get my records through the office, but they wouldn't release them to anyone except my court-appointed guardian. When I told them there was no way my aunt would come to Detroit, they said they'd mail them directly to the school. I was sunk if that happened. I knew if I broke in and took only*

*my file they'd figure out it was me. So I started a small fire to burn a couple of file drawers, figuring the sprinklers would kick in and put it out before there was any major damage. By the time they got around to replacing the files with duplicates from the main office there wouldn't be anyone who remembered they were supposed to send my records here."*

*"So what happened?"*

*"The sprinklers didn't work."*

*"And the whole school burned?"*

*"Not the whole school. The administration offices."*

*"Was anyone hurt?"*

*You shook your head. "But they made a big deal out of it on the news and in the newspapers the next day. Hell, you'd have thought I'd burned down the Pontiac Silverdome and that the Pistons had to play in the parking lot. Then it came out that this wasn't the first school fire that summer. The cops said whoever did this one did the others, too, and they had a serial arsonist on their hands. I decided that if I owned up to it, I'd get nailed for the others, too."*

*"We have to tell my dad."*

*"Shit, Julia—you promised."*

*"He won't tell anyone."*

*"But he'll know." You lowered your head, hiding your face with a waterfall of black hair. "Everything will change. It always does when people find out bad*

*things about you. They might want to forget, but they can't."*

*"My dad's not like that. He'll help you."*

*"No one can help me, Julia. I did it. Nothing anyone can say or do can change that."*

*That was when I did something I wanted to do since the day we met. I leaned over and kissed you. It wasn't a good kiss, landing more on your cheek than your lips, but you got the idea. I could see you struggling with what to do next. Then, with a deep moan that was like some kind of magnet that reached all the way to my heart, you pulled me into your arms and kissed me back.*

*I will remember that kiss until the day I die, Evan. Things melted in me that I never knew existed. It didn't matter that the gearshift was stuck in my ribs or that my body was twisted in ways it wasn't meant to twist; all I could think about, all I cared about, was finding a way to keep your lips from leaving mine.*

# CHAPTER 5

Julia poured another cup of coffee and headed back upstairs to finish packing. Shaking off a foolish, lingering unease over the phone call, she mentally recited the list of things she still had to do before Harold arrived.

At the landing she absently stopped to pick a piece of lint off the threadbare carpet. The night before Evan left for Colombia, he'd joked that their Christmas presents to each other that year would be five gallons of paint, their birthday presents new carpeting and for Valentine's Day a new stove.

At first she'd put off the major changes and repairs they'd talked about, waiting until he could be there to do them with her. Finally, one by one she'd gone ahead, convincing herself it was all right, that Evan wouldn't be coming home to a house he didn't recognize but to one with the changes they'd planned together. She'd finished the work two years ago, everything but the carpeting and the new stove. Those, for some unfathomable reason, she couldn't bring herself to do without him.

She'd instantly fallen in love with the house the Realtor had generously called a fixer-upper. Evan hadn't caught her enthusiasm until he saw the backyard. After sitting at the kitchen table at their old house, listing all the things they would have to do to make the new house livable and how much it would add to the cost, Julia accepted, reluctantly, that it was beyond their means. She continued to look at other houses in the area, bringing Evan into the search whenever she found something with potential, but it was like having a passion for French fries and being offered potato chips.

Nothing gave her the same emotional connection. It was something she couldn't explain. Through the tattered, garish wallpaper, the pink tile in the bathrooms, the ancient appliances in the kitchen, she saw the warmth in the exposed beam ceiling in the family room, the shine of refinished oak floors, the joy of friends and family gathered under the limbs of the hundred-year-old heritage oak in the backyard.

She had been ready to tell the Realtor to expand the search, moving from Carmichael to Fair Oaks, when Evan called one morning and told her to meet him for lunch at Venita Rhea's, their favorite restaurant in Rocklin and only five minutes from Stephens Engineering.

He'd phoned ahead and asked Randy to reserve their special table next to the mural, the one with the baby duck swimming in the canal. Evan said the expansive painting represented the French countryside; Julia said it had to be Italy. They could have settled the ongoing argument by asking Lisa, one of the owners, but that would have been too easy.

During dessert—an obscenely large and incredible bread pudding, which Evan had insisted they order in lieu of champagne—he'd handed her an exquisitely wrapped package. Inside was an offer on the house, lacking only her signature.

They visited the vacant house a dozen times in the month it took to close, planning, deciding which projects they work on first, which could be postponed. Her enthusiasm for the inside became his, while she grew more and more caught up with his ideas for the garden, picturing the four of them eating outside on the deck under the oak tree surrounded by a living rainbow.

They met at Venita Rhea's so often over the next month to go over kitchen-design brochures and paint chips and carpet samples that Julia put on three pounds.

The pounds came off the week they actually moved in, when they alternated between euphoria and exhaustion, eating off paper plates set on boxes, working until two in the morning to clean years of accumulated dirt in the kitchen and then getting up at six to work their paying jobs. They barely gave themselves time to stop and admire a finished room before moving on to the next. It was a perfect month, filled with dreams, with hope, with nonstop talk of the future. Words that still haunted her when she thought of everything Evan had missed.

Julia curled the retrieved piece of lint into a ball between her fingers and finished climbing the stairs. She was on her way to the bathroom to toss the lint in the trash when the phone rang. She hesitated. For an instant she considered letting it go to the answering machine, but was brought up short by her bizarre reaction. Not once in five years had she ever ignored a ringing telephone.

She answered in the bedroom.

"Hope I didn't catch you at a bad time," Harold said. The necessity to identify himself had disappeared years ago. "Something has come up that I have to take care of before we leave for the airport. Would it be all right if Mary swung by an hour earlier to pick you up first?" He was as involved with working to bring Evan home now as he had been in the beginning.

"Sure." And then she remembered. "I thought Mary was out of town."

"She came home last night."

Julia laughed. "Didn't trust you to pack for yourself?" Harold was notorious for his unusual taste in clothes. As her and Harold's and Mary's friendships had grown into something far past ordinary, Mary had gently tugged Julia out of several deep emotional holes with stories of Harold's lifelong fashion faux pas. She particularly loved the one about the Hawaiian shirt and pin-stripe suit combination he'd worn to a semiformal award ceremony, but had only personally witnessed his appearance at a company picnic in brown socks, loafers, rainbow-colored shorts and a turtleneck.

"Maybe, but she had the good grace to tell me it was because she missed me. Of course, she was going through my suitcase at the time, so I wasn't entirely convinced."

"Tell her I'll be ready."

"Thanks, Julia."

"No problem."

She glanced at the clock when she hung up and jumped when the phone instantly rang again. Five minutes to nine. Her mother. The two-hour time difference between California and Kansas put her mother between the work she did for the volunteer fire department on Wednesday and getting lunch ready for her father.

Julia tucked the receiver between her ear and shoulder and reached into a drawer for a shoe bag. "Hi, Mom."

First silence and then static filled the line.

Dropping the bag on the bed, she shifted the receiver to her hand. "Hello?" She waited. "Is anyone there?"

The line cleared. She heard a man say, "...twelve kilometers south of Envigado..." A series of clicks followed.

Envigado? She knew that name. It was a city in Colombia just south of Medellin. "Evan?" she said in a choked whisper. "Evan, is it you?" More clicks, and then a hum telling her she'd been disconnected.

She put the phone down and bumped the vase with the peach-colored rose. A petal fell. Her breath caught. Seconds passed as she stood there and stared. She absolutely refused to see it as a sign. She couldn't live that way. The rose was old and fragile, and freeze-dried flowers weren't meant to last forever.

*Damn it, Mother. Why have you done this to me?*

She headed for the computer in Jason's room to look up Envigado's exact location. The phone rang again.

Her heart in her throat, she answered. "What is it? What are you trying to tell me?"

"Julia?" her mother said hesitantly. "Is that you?"

Julia sat on the corner of the bed. "I thought you were someone else."

"Obviously. What's wrong?"

"Nothing." If she told her mother about the strange phone calls, she would either say Julia was cracking up or that it was another sign. Julia wasn't up to dealing with either possibility. "It's been a busy morning and I'm feeling a little on edge about the meeting with this new ambassador."

"It sounded like something more than that."

"Really, it's nothing."

"All right. I was just checking up on you, and wanted to tell you I had a dream about Evan last night. You two were sitting in the backyard in those special chairs you bought to celebrate his birthday last year."

"Adirondack," Julia said.

"You were so happy," her mother continued. "I woke up and I was crying. I asked everyone at church to say a prayer that this new ambassador will be able to do something."

"Thanks, Mom." Even with call waiting she was reluctant to stay on the phone any longer. "I have to let you go so I can finish packing."

"Don't forget your raincoat."

"I won't."

"Did Barbara stop by this morning?"

"She did."

"And?" Maggie prompted.

"She gave me the clover. I have it in my purse. Now, I really do have to go."

Two hours and six phone calls later, Julia had managed to convince herself that the strange call was simply another Colombian reporter looking for a new angle for a five-year anniversary story about the longest-held American kidnap victim. She had dressed and finished packing and was on her way downstairs, suitcase in hand, when the phone rang yet again. Mentally going over the list of friends and family who had yet to contact her, she settled on her brother.

After five years it was more than reasonable to expect her friends and family to have shifted focus and moved past the intensity of waiting to hear something about Evan's kidnapping, which had gripped them all in the beginning. But Evan was still almost as much a part of their lives as he was hers. For a long time she'd believed their continued intimate involvement was because they loved and cared about her. And they did. But it was Evan himself who drew their hopes and concerns and prayers. They refused to believe a heart so filled with love and compassion and joy no longer beat.

Instead of the expected baritone of her brother, Fred, she was greeted by a woman's voice. "Mrs. Julia McDonald, please."

"Speaking."

"Please hold for Mr. Leland Crosby."

"I'm sorry—who did you say?"

"Mr. Leland Crosby," she repeated carefully.

Before Julia could say anything in response, he came on the line. "Leland Crosby here, Mrs. McDonald. I'm sure you don't remember me, but we met when you were in Washington a couple of years ago."

"I'm sorry, I don't—"

"Please, don't apologize. There's no reason for you to remember. I was one of a dozen diplomats you met that day. But since Paul Erickson was out of the office today and you and I did have that connection, I wanted to be the one to call you personally to offer my condolences and to let you know that our ambassador's office in Colombia will do everything possible to help you in any way they can."

"Condolences?" she repeated numbly. "I don't understand."

Agonizingly long seconds passed. "No one has contacted you? You don't know?"

"Know what?"

"Just a moment, please." She couldn't make out what was said next, but the angry tone clearly made it through the muffled receiver. "I'm truly sorry, Mrs. McDonald. I was told the Colombian authorities had already contacted you, that you'd already been informed."

"Informed about what?" she demanded.

"Your husband."

Her hand tightened around the receiver. "Evan?" Panic squeezed her chest. She fought to take a breath. "Is he all right?" How could he be? No one offered condolences when someone was rescued. Still, she could not accept that Evan was gone until she heard the actual words.

"I'm so sorry. Is there anyone there with you?" He waited, and when she didn't answer, "Is there someone I can call?"

*"Is he all right?"*

After a long pause, with great reluctance, Leland Crosby said, "The Colombian army found your husband two days ago…in a shallow grave with two other men."

Still she clung to her belief that Evan was alive, that he was waiting for her, loving her, missing her, holding on to life when it would be easier to let go, because he knew that if he died, a part of her, the best part of her, would die, too. This core knowledge had sustained her for five years. "Are you sure it's him?"

"I'm going to let you talk to someone else about that, someone who can give you answers that I can't." Before passing the phone, he added, "I realize this is a difficult time for you. You have my deepest sympathy."

She didn't want his sympathy. She wanted answers.

"Thank you," she answered automatically, hanging on to a piece of fragile silk thread as if it were a steel cable.

A new voice came on the line. "Hello—Mrs. McDonald?"

"Yes."

"This is Roger Hopkins. I understand you have some questions for me."

She pressed herself into the corner where the kitchen and dining room met, and clung to the wall for support. She didn't have to ask her questions; she could just hang up, go on with her morning, waiting for the call telling her there had been a mistake, that it wasn't Evan they'd found but someone who looked like him.

"Mrs. McDonald—are you there?"

*Please, please let it be a nightmare. Let me be asleep, let something happen to wake me and make it all go away.* Evan couldn't be dead. Not now. Not after all this time.

Forcing words past the lump in her throat, she struggled to ask, "How do they know it's Evan?"

"The forensic pathologist in Bogotá had a copy of his medical and dental records…and there were several personal belongings recovered."

"What kind of personal belongings?"

"His wallet and watch." He paused. "And a wedding ring with the words *Spring to Winter* written inside. According to the information you supplied when Mr. McDonald went missing, this was the inscription on his wedding band."

She closed her eyes. Her knees gave out and she slid along the wall until she was sitting on the floor. "When?"

"Pardon me?"

"When did he die?" She wanted to look back, to remember where she was, what she'd been doing when it had happened. She believed without question that his last thought would be of her and his children. He would have reached out to her to say goodbye. Had she been too caught up in creating a newsletter for a client, or cheering at a soccer game, or rushing to catch a plane to hear him?

"According to the man who led them to the grave, Evan was shot trying to escape two days after he was captured."

A sharp pain cut through her chest. "No-o-o-o..." She doubled over and pressed herself deeper into the corner. "That can't be. I would have known."

"I'm really sorry you had to learn about this over the phone. We were assured the authorities in Colombia had contacted you this morning and made arrangements for someone to be with you."

*They'd tried. They just hadn't gotten through.* "I think I'm going to hang up now." She spoke slowly, her composure a bridge that had lost its foundation. Understanding that once she let go she would not be able to function, she asked one last question. "Who should I contact to find out when they'll be releasing Evan?"

"As I understand it, you'll have to go through the coroner's office first. Someone will have to interpret for you."There was a sound of shuffling papers."The doctor doesn't speak English."

"I know Spanish." She'd immersed herself in the language and in the country, believing knowledge was power. For five years she'd studied. She'd learned as much about the history and traditions and social structure of Colombia as she had her own country. Maybe more.

And now, with one phone call on a clear January day, she'd been told all she'd ever really needed was a satin-lined casket and a one-way ticket.

"I don't seem to have the phone number for the doctor in front of me," he told her. "I don't want to keep you on the line while I look. Would it be all right if I called you back in a few minutes?"

"I'll need the contact number for the Colombian office that will release Evan to let him come home."

"Of course. Will you excuse me for a moment?" When he returned, he said, "We can have the embassy make those arrangements for you, Mrs. McDonald."

"When?"

"I'll have them get in touch with you."

"Make sure Ambassador Sidney is told that I want to be with Evan when he comes home."

"I understand."

"But you have to make sure they understand, too."

She'd experienced too many well-intentioned mistakes. Messages weren't always delivered as they were intended.

"I'll take care of it. I promise."

"Thank you," she said. She would contact them, too. There was only one thing left that she could do for Evan. Propriety be damned.

"Again, let me express my profound sorrow," he said. "For everything."

She put her hand over her eyes and bit her lip. "I have to go now."

"Are you sure there isn't anyone I could call?"

"No—" She dropped the receiver and covered her face with both hands. A deep, keening sob echoed through the empty house.

How could Evan have been dead for five years when his favorite cereal was in the cupboard, his clothes in the closet, his dresser filled with his underwear and socks and T-shirts, all waiting for him? How could he come to her in her dreams with tender promises of what their lives would be like when they were together again? How could she be standing at the sink, washing dishes, or driving the car, or talking on the phone, or working in the yard, and feel him beside her and know without question that he was thinking about her and telling her that she was loved beyond barriers or miles or time?

How could she go on without the belief he was

waiting for her to find him? How could she get up in the morning knowing she had to get through another day without hope?

*Four Months and Two Weeks Missing*

*We found my dad in the barn, sharpening a lawnmower blade. He had his back to us, oblivious to everything in the isolation of the high-pitched whine of the grinder and the goggles he wore to protect his eyes from the wildly flying sparks. I could feel your tension as we stood there waiting for him to finish; you really didn't want to be there. You were scared. And there was nothing I could say or do to reassure you.*

*I reached for your hand and you jumped. It was then that I realized the depth of your fear and how important my father had become to you. For seventeen years you had lived in an environment that should have destroyed you. When you took over the care of your brother, you missed so much school that you sacrificed the dream of graduating high enough in your class to get a scholarship to college. And then when he died so uselessly, you'd suffered loss I couldn't conceive. Yet you not only hung on, you survived without anger or bitterness. I'd never known anyone like you. Your core goodness left me awestruck.*

*Finally, Dad noticed us and flipped the switch on the grinder. He removed his goggles and flashed us a smile. When it wasn't eagerly returned, he wiped his hands on the rag sticking out of his overalls pocket and motioned us closer. "What's up?"*

*You shoved your hands in your back pockets and*

*tilted your head down, escaping in the shadows of your hair. "Julia thinks I should...Julia wants me to—" You looked up then and must have seen something in my father's eyes that made it all right, because you took a deep breath and blurted out, "I'm a fugitive, Mr. Warren. I'm wanted for setting a fire in my old school. I didn't mean for it to happen, but that's not going to count for shit to the cops when they catch me."*

*Not exactly the way I'd pictured it happening. I mentally braced myself and waited for the explosion.*

*My dad shifted from one foot to the other. "That's the ice that's above the water. I want to see what's underneath before I pass judgment."*

*I'd always believed my father the strongest most honorable man alive, someone who taught his children compassion and fairness by example. I'd never been more proud to be his daughter than I was at that moment. I glanced at you and said softly, "See?" I grinned. "I told you."*

*You repeated your story in an emotionless voice, as if reading an article from the newspaper about someone you'd never met. It was plain you didn't want his pity or mine and that you were there only because I'd asked you.*

*My father was shaken, his face a mirror of his thoughts as he went from anger to sorrow. "I knew there was something special about you the first time we met," he said. "I just had no idea how special you really were." He put his hand on your shoulder. "I just might be able to help you out with this fire business. Give me a couple of weeks."*

*You tried hard to hide them, but there were tears in your eyes when you said, "I don't see how—"*

*"I'm not making any promises, Evan. I'll do what I can. But in the meantime there's something I have to have from you." He looked at me. "And you."*

*"I'll do anything, Daddy." And I would have. "I'll even take the night shift on the combine next summer."*

*He chuckled. "Don't think I won't remember you saying that come harvest time." And then to Evan, "Seems to me that we've got our work cut out for us if we're going to get you caught up by graduation. Julia, you're going back to riding the bus and getting your own homework done before supper. Evan, you'll go back to working with Mrs. Winslow on the English after school, and then Julia and I will alternate with algebra and social studies until you're where you should be. Julia's mom has four years of high-school German and three of college. If you have any ear at all for foreign languages, she can get you to the point where you can challenge the course for credit. I'm not usually in favor of this kind of thing, but you'll need a language when you apply for college yourself."*

*I threw my arms around his neck. "Daddy, I love you. You're the best."*

*"Why are you doing this?" you asked, confused at a reaction you obviously hadn't expected.*

*"For a lot of reasons," Dad said. "Mostly, I suppose, because I think it's about time you were on the receiving end. You're a good kid, Evan. All you need is half a chance."*

*"I don't know what to say."*

*"One more thing," Dad said, seeing we were about to leave. He shifted his gaze from me to you and then back again. "It's plain as a cat locked in a house watching a flock of birds in the backyard how you two feel about each other." He held up his hand when I started to protest. "I've got eyes, Julia. Anyone around you two five minutes would pick up on what's going on between you. I just don't want it getting out of hand. You've got plenty of time. Right now Evan has enough on his plate."*

*I looked into your eyes and could see the yearning for everything my father had offered mixed with a longing for me. The promise we made to my dad that day to stay away from each other was one of the hardest promises I've ever made. But I sucked it up, as Fred liked to say, and smiled. I wanted you to know that it was okay. I would wait.*

# CHAPTER 6

The doorbell rang. Julia ignored it. It rang again. Julia pulled her legs to her chest and leaned tighter into the corner. Loud knocking came next, and then a man called her name.

"Mrs. McDonald?" He knocked again. "This is Deputy Thompson from the Sheriff's Department. Are you all right in there?"

Julia stirred. He'd obviously been sent to see her and would not go away until she responded.

"Mrs. McDonald? Can you—"

"Just a minute," she finally said. She got to her feet, wiped her face with her hands and adjusted her skirt. She was experienced at hiding her feelings, smiling when she was exhausted, speaking softly when she felt like shouting, gracious when inwardly seething with frustration. Grief, worry, fear were all emotions she'd learned to bury under a veneer of cordialness, a necessary means to an end.

She glanced at herself in the hall mirror before opening the door. Her eyes betrayed her. She could not hide behind a smile today; the wound ran too deep. Still, she tried. "I'm Julia McDonald," she said. "What can I do for you?"

A young man dressed in crisp Sheriff's Department green, with a shiny badge and buttons, a wide, black leather belt and bulging holster, took a nervous half step backward. He had bright-red hair and connect-the-dots freckles and looked years too young to have a gun strapped at his side. Another man, dressed in a black suit and cleric's collar, stood with one foot on the step, the other on the porch. He seemed disconcertingly familiar with the role he'd been assigned.

The deputy shifted his hat from one hand to the other, radiating vibes that said, given a choice, he would gladly take an armed suspect over a distraught woman. He cleared his throat. "I'm sorry to disturb you at a time like this, Mrs. McDonald, but Mayor Suhr's office received a phone call from the State Department requesting an officer be sent to this address. Reverend Kistler and I are here to help you in any way we can."

"Thank you," Julia said. "I appreciate the mayor's concern, but I really don't need help. There's nothing for you to do."

"Please, ma'am—there must be something."

"Perhaps we could phone a friend?" Reverend Kistler suggested. "What about family? Do you have any close by?"

Reality pierced her fog of sorrow. No matter how desperately she wanted to be left alone, to grieve in private, to say goodbye to Evan in the quiet of the house they had shared in dreams but not time, there were others who had to be considered. "My sister, Barbara."

They reacted as if she'd given them a gift. "If we could come inside..." Reverend Kistler gently suggested.

"Of course." She moved out of the doorway. "Would you like some coffee?" The question was automatic, inbred through generations of women who equated food and drink with hospitality even in grief, women who throughout joy and tragedy passed the lesson to their daughters by example.

She could do this; she could go on, alone. After five years without being able to see or feel or touch Evan, she'd already accomplished it physically. Now all she had to do was find a way to do it mentally. One step at a time, one day at a time, and it would become a pattern.

Knowing Evan would never come home was simply a matter of trading one heartache for another.

Within an hour, the rippling word of Evan's death had reached friends across the United States and Colombia. One conversation ended, the receiver was replaced, the phone rang again. Barbara handled all but the most personal calls, noting names and numbers and thanking all for their concern, promising someone would get back to them as soon as the funeral arrangements were made.

Julia listened the way she did with background music, hearing, but not registering details. She remained at the front window, her hand pressed against the cool glass, and watched for Shelly and Jason.

She'd heard from Paul Erickson and George Black and Matt Coatney, the men who'd begun the battle to get Evan home and then over the years had moved on to other jobs in other businesses and agencies. Five years was a long time for men like that to stay in one place.

Not one of them hinted that they'd ever lost hope, and in their voices and words, she felt their shared sorrow. They all told her they would stay in touch, but their link had been severed. Even friendships formed in the fires of adversity suffered and fell to the wayside when not tended regularly.

In less than an hour the sun had given way to a

cover of dark clouds, dropping the temperature ten degrees. White-crowned sparrows and juncos popped in and out of the perennial bed next to the driveway, their food gathering hastened by the impending rain.

The perennials were Evan's favorites, everything from foxglove to primroses. In the backyard she'd planted hundreds of daffodils and tulips in meandering beds of yellow and red, deep purple and white, the colors he had marked in the bulb catalog he'd left on the nightstand.

She'd painted the house his favorite colors, wallpapered the bathroom in the pattern he'd said he'd liked when they were at the store together the week before he left, and covered the windows with the miniblinds he preferred instead of the wooden plantation shutters she liked. They were labors of love, small bargains that her efforts would not go unnoticed, that someday Evan would take pleasure in the paint and paper and pick her a bouquet from the garden.

The sky behind the Modesto ash in the front yard lit with a flash of lightning. Julia waited for the thunder. Rain fell, gently at first, and then as if the clouds had tilted to drop their contents as quickly as possible.

*How could she have not known?* The question reverberated like an echo. How could she have felt Evan's presence all those years, when he hadn't been with her anymore?

The answer finally struck, and it was cold and hard and cruel. She'd believed because she had to. Without the fantasy, she could not have done what she had to do.

And in the end, she had succeeded. She had found him.

Julia glanced up as Patty's Mustang pulled into the driveway. Shelly sat in the front passenger seat talking, her face animated, her gestures expansive. She seemed happy, excited, her world as it should be, filled with friends and flights of fancy. She would recover from losing her father—she'd had five years of practice. But she would be changed. She would miss the connection that was part of knowing there was another person in her world who loved her without reservation.

They would have no more conversations about what it would be like when Evan came home. He would never see the trophies she'd won for soccer or the ornaments she'd made for him each Christmas. She would look into the stands at her graduation from high school and college and see her grandfather where her father should have been. And when she walked down the aisle at her wedding, no matter who walked with her it would be the wrong person.

As if she could sense Julia waiting for her, Shelly turned and saw her mother. Her smile faded. She gathered her books and left the car. After taking a second to wave goodbye, she sprinted toward the house, futilely attempting to outrun the rain.

Julia met her at the door.

"What are you doing here?" Shelly asked. "I thought your plane—"

"The trip was canceled." Julia took Shelly's books and put them on the hall table.

"Then why is Aunt Barbara here?" She shrugged out of her coat. "What's going on?"

Julia had given her children every kind of news and not struggled for words. Now, suddenly, she had no idea what to say. Was there a right way to break someone's heart? "They found—"

"Daddy?" Shelly finished for her, her eyes brimming with anticipation.

Julia panicked, realizing Shelly completely misunderstood and would suffer the blow twice.

"Where?" Shelly added before Julia could react.

"In the jungle outside Envigado," she said, supplying the wrong answer and allowing the fantasy to live.

"When is he coming home?" She didn't wait for Julia to answer. "Why aren't you happy?"

"He isn't coming home...not to us. At least not the way we wanted him to." She was doing this all wrong. "Your father is dead, Shelly." It sounded so cruel. She should have thought more about how to lessen the blow.

Shelly's jacket fell to the floor. "How do you know?" And then, "How did it happen?"

The question threw Julia. And then she remembered. She couldn't tell Shelly the truth, not after what she'd said that morning about wishing her father had been shot.

Barbara moved into the hall. "He was shot attempting to escape—just a couple of days after he was captured," she added gently, obviously believing she was helping. "He's been gone all this time. We should have known your father wouldn't sit around waiting for someone to rescue him."

Shelly stared at Julia, her eyes wide in horror. "That's not true. It can't be. You're making it up." She backed into the wall, trying to get away. "Why would you do that to me? I told you I was sorry."

"This has nothing to do with you." Julia took Shelly's arm. "It's an ugly coincidence. That's all."

Shelly twisted out of her grasp. "You don't know that," she shouted. "You can't."

"What's going on?" Barbara asked. "What did I do?"

"Nothing," Julia told her, focusing on Shelly.

Shelly let out a wail. She turned to Barbara, a beseeching look in her eyes. "This morning I told Mom…I told her…I wished they'd shot Daddy a long time ago." She brought her hands up in a helpless gesture. "It's my fault."

"Stop it, Shelly," Julia said. "Think about what you're saying. You know that can't possibly be true."

Barbara took her in her arms, casting a helpless look in Julia's direction. "Oh, honey, don't do this to yourself. You only said what all of us have thought at one time or another."

Julia recoiled. In that moment she hated her sister. The idea that Evan's death would bring relief to anyone was almost more than she could bear. She had never, not in her most desperately lonely moments, wished herself free of the effort to bring him home. She'd been willing to spend the rest of her life waiting. She was still willing.

The phone rang. Barbara glanced toward the kitchen.

"I'll get it," Julia said. She was afraid to say anything to Barbara and wasn't ready to say the words Shelly needed to hear. Until she could, it was better to leave them to each other's care.

The man on the phone was a florist asking where to deliver flowers. She gave him her address and then regretted it. She couldn't face the cloying smell of funeral arrangements or the accompanying trappings of death. It was too soon. She had to have more time.

The doorbell rang. She moved to answer it, when the phone rang again. Momentarily ignoring it, she stepped to the window. Harold and Mary were at the front door, his eyes red and swollen, his shoulders stooped, Mary clutching a casserole dish as if it were a lifeline. A movement at the end of the driveway caught her eye. Oblivious to the extra cars parked out front, Jason and Tom joked and jabbed and moseyed along the walkway up to the house, disregarding the rain.

Julia felt as though she was being parceled out piece by piece to the people who counted on her. She had to find a way to save a part of herself for Evan. What did it matter that she would have nothing left? She had the rest of her life to become whole again.

The plane rattled and creaked and roared as it raced down the runway before lifting with a stomach-lurching leap. After three days in Bogotá, Julia was finally headed for home again. Acknowledging she would never return to Colombia, she'd arranged time to see and thank the friends she'd made over the years, the officials who had stuck with her long after everyone else had given up and Matt Coatney, who was there on another hostage negotiation and had unexpectedly knocked on her hotel door late one night. The hardened negotiator sat with his back bowed, his hands on his knees, and fought to keep from breaking down as he talked about the hope he'd had that despite the years that had gone by without hearing from the kidnappers, Evan would one day walk out of the jungle and go home to Julia.

When asked if she felt it would help her to talk to the man who had led police to the grave site, she'd declined at first and then changed her mind. She'd imagined a seasoned man, hard and uncompromising. He was young and terrified. He hadn't witnessed Evan being shot, but he'd dug the grave and heard the story of the attempted escape. At the time he'd been in his early teens, only a year older than Jason was now.

The comparison made it impossible for her to hate him. She'd sought a focus for her anger and instead found herself weighed down by the evidence of a wasted life.

The airplane's wheels thumped into place and they began a slow, banked turn, heading north. Heading home.

Minutes later they cleared the clouds and the plane leveled. A flight attendant arrived, a smile in place. Julia declined the beverage offer and turned to face the window.

She'd imagined flying home with Evan a hundred times, picturing them holding hands, caught up in each other and oblivious to everything and everyone around them. He would laugh when she told him about the hundreds of carpet samples awaiting him at home, and she would cry when he told her how lonely he'd been without her. They would not be able to stop looking at each other. She pictured her hand on his cheek, the feel of his breath as he touched his lips to hers, a sweet warmth spreading through her body as he whispered that he loved her.

She wouldn't have to tell him how desperately she had missed him or how hard she had worked to bring him home. He would know this as surely as he knew she would have waited for him forever.

He would gaze at pictures of Shelly and Jason with wonder and surprise at how they'd grown. She would tell him how Jason had broken his arm when he'd tumbled out of the oak tree while reattaching the bird feeder that had fallen in a storm, and how Shelly had scored the winning goal in the district soccer championship.

She closed her eyes and tried to imagine him beside her, breathing the sharp, clean air of freedom and luxuriating in the comfort of flying first class.

But the reality of accompanying him to the airport that morning, of standing beside the plane as his casket was loaded into the baggage compartment, of the subtle, careful manipulations to keep curious onlookers away, was too powerful to allow her this last, small fantasy.

When they arrived in San Francisco, Evan would be the last to depart the plane. A hearse would take him the final ninety miles to Sacramento and he would spend the night in the mortuary, alone. Two days later they would say their formal goodbyes during the service Barbara had arranged at their parish church.

Everything was in place. There was nothing more for her to do, no magic wand to ease the pain or lessen the sorrow. No way to change that one moment in time when Evan had decided to risk everything to come home to her.

In another week the relatives would be gone, Shelly and Jason would be back in school, Barbara would be back at work and Julia would be doing whatever she could find to fill her day.

And Evan would be in the ground. Alone.

Holding her breath against the pain, Julia reached into her purse and removed the manila envelope the clerk at the pathologist's office had given her. She hadn't been able to bring herself to look inside at the "personal belongings" recovered with Evan—his wallet, his watch, a gift from her on their tenth anniversary, his wedding ring. They'd told her the money and credit cards were missing, but a driver's license and several photographs of her and Shelly and Jason had survived the burial.

She hugged the envelope against her chest. Slow, silent tears slid down her cheeks.

*Five Months and Two Weeks Missing*

*The whole family pitched in to get you through your senior year. I handled the English, my dad math, Mom made you learn way more than you needed to pass civics and challenge German and Fred let you slide in biology until Barbara took over. Someone in the office decided that since your records were lost, the best thing to do was average your grades over all four years, and you wound up in the top ten percent of the class. Dad nearly burst his buttons at our graduation.*

*You spent so much time at the house that year that Dad put another bed in Fred's room so you didn't have to sleep on the couch. After being with you all day at school and then all night at home, keeping our promise to my dad was like putting a field mouse in front of a barn cat and telling the cat to play nice.*

*In January when Dad took you aside and told you that in exchange for dropping the arson charges you were to spend the next four summers in your old neighborhood in Detroit, tutoring disadvantaged kids, I was thrilled that you'd escaped a trial and possible jail time. Of course summer seemed a long time off when there was a blizzard blowing outside and we were still putting away the Christmas decorations.*

*Graduation was hard on me. All I could think about was that you were leaving in a week and that for a year you'd be at the community college twenty miles away from the farm, while I'd be at the University of Kansas, half a state away. To say that I was unhappy was like saying a lead weight didn't float.*

*The day before you were supposed to leave I got up early and packed a picnic lunch for us. I loaded it and my grandmother's old quilt in the back of the truck, and the minute you came downstairs I grabbed your arm and hauled you out the front door.*

*As soon as we pulled out of the driveway, I scooted across the seat and snuggled into your side. "Where are we headed?" you asked.*

*"Someplace no one will find us."*

*You didn't answer right away. "I don't know, Julia. The way I've been feeling lately I don't think that's such a good idea."*

*"You're worried about your promise to my dad," I guessed, hoping I was right because it was what I wanted to hear.*

*"Yes."*

*"That's over, Evan."*

*"How do you figure?"*

*"We said we wouldn't do anything while you were staying at the house. You're leaving tomorrow. What possible harm is one day going to do?"*

*"He trusts me, Julia. I can't do anything to mess that up."*

*"And what about me?"*

*You pulled over to the side of the road, skidded to a stop and turned in the seat, glaring at me. "You don't have a clue. If you did, you could never ask me such a stupid question. Do you really not know how I feel about you? Is this some game to you?"*

*"I'm sorry." I wasn't, not really, but I couldn't think of anything to say. In all the imagining and planning I'd done getting ready for this day, not once had it happened this way. "I just want to be with you."*

*"And you imagine I haven't been half out of my mind lately wanting to be with you? Are you blind?"*

*That did it. I was in your arms kissing you, and you were kissing me back, and I was feeling heat and yearning in parts of me I hardly knew existed.*

*A car drove by and the driver honked at us. I looked up and realized it was our neighbor, the woman my mother said didn't need a mouth to spread gossip; it oozed out her pores.*

*"Where?" you asked.*

*"What about that sycamore with the nest of raccoons?"*

*"Behind the wheat field?"*

*"I heard Dad tell Fred that he was going to town for a meeting at the bank. And there isn't any reason for anyone else to be out there today."*

*You took my hand and kissed it. I was sure I was ten seconds away from melting into a puddle on the floor. There was no way we could get where we were going fast enough. I wanted you and I didn't want to wait another minute.*

*"Are you sure about this, Julia?*

*"Yes. Yes, yes, yes," I shouted.*

*Still you hesitated. "I don't have anything, any kind of protection."*

*"I do," I admitted sheepishly. I hadn't been sure how I was going to bring up the fact that I had a condom in my purse, and now I didn't have to. All I knew was that I wasn't going to spend the day with you unprepared for what I desperately wanted to happen.*

*"Where did you—"*

*"It's Fred's."*

*"What?"*

*"I was putting his laundry away and there it was. Actually, there were lots of them. I only took one. He'll never miss it."*

*"It was just sitting there in his drawer, where you or your mom could find it?"*

*"Well, not exactly. I had to do a little looking around."*

*"How did you know what they were?"*

*"Oh, please. What do you think I am, some Barbie doll that's been left in its package for seventeen years?"*

*"I know exactly what you are—all mouth. You're no more experienced at this sex thing than I am."*

*I was stunned and didn't even try to hide it. "You mean you've never? Not once?"*

*"Does that bother you?"*

*"It surprises me, that's all."*

*"Why?"*

*"I guess it's because you're a guy. Look at Fred. He's two years younger than you and—"*

*"You don't really believe he's doing anything where he needs all those condoms, do you?"*

*"Why have them if you're not going to use them?"*

*"God—you're such a girl."*

*"What's that got to do with anything?"*

*"Someday I'll tell you about guys. Or at least, I'll try. No promises."*

*"Why didn't you? I mean, you must have had a hundred girls chasing you when you lived in Detroit."*

*"Why would you believe that? Look around, Julia. Do you see any girls chasing me here?" He grinned. "Present company excepted."*

*I laughed at that. "Are you serious? The only reason you didn't have half the girls in the school following you around with their tongues hanging out was that I let them know I wouldn't put up with it."*

*"So does all this questioning mean you'd prefer someone more experienced your first time?"*

*"When I went to all the trouble to get this?" I held up the condom.*

*You laughed. "You realize Fred would kill you if he found out you were going through his things."*

*I grinned. "Who's going to tell him?"*

*You put your hand on the back of my neck and brought me close for another kiss. "Sure as hell not me."*

# CHAPTER 7

Abandoning her futile effort at sleep, Julia got out of bed at the first light of dawn and went outside to watch the sunrise. Six months had passed since she'd brought Evan home and it seemed like yesterday. How many more months would it take for the healing to begin? How many years? Would she live that long?

She stood on the porch and stared at the unfamiliar surroundings, at the lake, the towering pines standing like ghostly sentinels at the edge of the dew-covered grass, at the pier that disappeared into the early-morning fog covering the lake.

At home she had the mindlessness of television

to keep her company when she couldn't sleep. She had hoped books would provide the escape she was looking for, but last night she'd found it no easier to concentrate in the mountains than it had been in the city.

Cold penetrated her knit leggings. She sat on the split-log railing and brought her baggy sweatshirt over her knees. Leaning her back against the porch pillar, she tried to picture Harold and Mary vacationing here, which they told her they'd done every summer when their kids were home but could no longer find the time to do. They'd left unspoken the reason there hadn't been time.

Mary had finally talked her into coming by insisting she would be doing them a favor, even if she only stayed a couple of weeks.

The grief counselor had told her Shelly and Jason needed to get away, to be somewhere free of memories, somewhere they could just be kids again. Implied in the suggestion was a need for them to get away from her for a while. So when her mother and father had suggested Shelly and Jason spend the summer with them on the farm and they'd responded as if they'd been offered tickets to a Dixie Chicks' concert, Julia had agreed to let them go. Reluctantly.

They might require time away from her, but she could hardly bear the thought of being away from them. They'd been gone less than a week and it seemed an eternity. She had no idea how she would make it through the summer alone.

A tree squirrel cautiously moved to the tip of a branch on the Jeffry pine at the end of the porch. It surveyed its world, spotted Julia and chattered a noisy alarm. A Steller's jay hopped to a nearby branch to see what the fuss was about. It cocked its head in Julia's direction, swooped down and landed in the middle of the lawn, looking at her expectantly.

"Sorry," Julia said. "I didn't think to bring birdseed. You'll have to wait until I get back from the store this afternoon."

One by one other sounds broke the stillness—the high-pitched chirp of a chipmunk, a low whisper of wind in the tops of pine and fir trees, a pine cone bouncing off branches on its way to the forest floor. Minor intrusions into the peace and quiet and solitude she was there to experience. The cure-all everyone had insisted was what she needed for her broken heart.

What no one understood was that her heart wasn't just broken; it was empty—something far worse. The passion that had driven her from bed every morning was gone. She drifted through her days, micro-managing the lives of two independent and self-sufficient teenagers, who vacillated between tolerance and rebellion.

She was just so sad all the time. She'd cried more

in the past six months than she'd cried the entire five years Evan was missing. She didn't want to be this way. She wanted to be stronger, to go on with her life the way she absolutely knew Evan would want her to, but she couldn't pull together the pieces that would let her look at her future and not see a lifetime of aching loneliness. She'd learned how to be alone; she had no idea how to be lonely.

The cold, damp air finally made its way through her sweatshirt. She shivered, stretched and went inside to make coffee, leaving the sunrise for another morning when she'd dressed warmer.

The "cabin" had been built in the twenties, when people of means escaped the Sacramento Valley's summer heat by fleeing to the mountains. Made out of logs and stone, it had a wide, covered porch that faced the lake and was the equivalent of the lavish vacation homes constructed at the turn of the century at Lake Tahoe. Surrounded by dense forest on three sides, the four hundred acres still owned by the Stephens' family backed up to land held in trust by the Nature Conservancy. The nearest neighbor was two miles away; the nearest town, almost twenty; the Oregon border, less than fifty. Mount Shasta was to the southeast; the coastal city of Eureka, a hundred miles or so to the southwest.

An expanse of tended lawn went from the house to the rocky shoreline of the lake, open room for a game of croquet or volleyball. It really was a shame no one came here anymore.

Despite this, the inside was as carefully and lovingly maintained as the outside, kept that way by the wife of a local fishing guide. Craftsman-style sofas and chairs upholstered in maroon and green fabrics sat in front of a large stone fireplace. The walls held original watercolors of local wildlife; an oil of Mount Shasta in its winter glory hung above the mantel.

The bedrooms were upstairs, five of them, each with bedspreads and curtains in fabrics popular in the twenties. Beautiful, handmade rag rugs protected the polished pine floors, stepping-stones of warmth on cold mornings.

She'd chosen the bedroom with the view of the lake. For almost half her life she'd made decisions based on what she believed Evan would want. Were he with her, they would be in the back bedroom, the one the sun would hit first in the morning, calling him to start his day. He loved the sunrise above all times of day, and would watch in rapt attention as the sky turned from black to purple to shot with gold. He said it was a renewal, the slate wiped clean, a chance to begin again.

She had never known anyone who loved life as much as Evan.

Julia went into the kitchen and opened the box of

supplies she'd brought, basic things to last until she could get to the grocery store. She started the coffee and then got her jacket from the bedroom. By the time she came back down the coffee was ready.

She chose the largest mug, filled it to the top with the steaming, dark liquid and went outside again. Settling on the top step this time, the mug warming her hands, she stared at the dock, or what she could see of it.

Her eyes softly focused, her mind lost in memories, she was slow to register the dark shadow that appeared in the gray mist at the end of the dock. Her eyes narrowed in concentration. What…?

The shadow moved. It was a man. Her heart did a quick, panicked dance when she heard his boots striking the rough planking and realized he was coming toward her. After leaving her parents' farm she'd become a city girl, the fear of strangers as elemental as navigating freeways.

He came nearer and she saw his red plaid shirt, his Giants baseball cap…his fishing pole.

*The caretaker.*

Feeling like an idiot, her heart still beating as if she'd run a marathon, she sat perfectly still, hoping he wouldn't notice her.

The man reached the end of the dock, hesitated, looked longingly to his left, and then with a slumped-shoulder show of resignation headed her way.

"I didn't think you'd be up this early," he said, stopping several feet from the porch.

He was near enough for her to notice black hair on the long side of neat and lightly graying at the temples. She figured him to be a few years older than her, though not many. But then, she'd never been good at guessing people's ages. His eyes were dark and deep set, with fine lines at the corners. And he was taller than he'd appeared at a distance, but not as large. He seemed as if he belonged in this setting, a little on the raw side, able to take in stride whatever vagaries nature delivered. The kind of man you would want with you in a crisis.

"You knew I was here?" She hadn't seen any signs that anyone was around when she'd arrived, no lights or smoke from a fireplace.

"We're too far from the main road to pick up traffic noises so it's pretty obvious when someone arrives."

"And here I thought I was being so quiet." She stood and held out her hand. "Julia McDonald."

He shifted his pole to the hand with the stringer of fish, leaned forward and clasped her outstretched hand. "David Prescott." He smiled. For an instant his face was transformed and he went from ruggedly competent to heart-stoppingly handsome. Julia took this in the way she observed most things, with a detached wonder.

"I had the impression you were—I thought you'd be older." She wished she'd asked Mary more about him.

"We reclusive types usually are, I guess."

"Yeah...I guess."

He shifted position and made a move to leave. "If you need anything, my place is a hundred yards, give or take, through those trees."

"Thanks." There was enough reluctance in the invitation that Julia smiled. Knowing he was content to keep his distance made it easier to be sociable.

"I just put on a pot of coffee. Would you like a cup?" she asked on impulse. *Now, where had that come from?*

He had the good graces to act as though he was considering her offer. "Thanks, maybe another time." He held up the trout on the stringer. "When I come back empty-handed."

She nodded, relieved. "Another time it is."

She went inside and phoned her mother. "Just thought I'd check in," she said. "I got here too late last night to call." Even with the kids in residence, her mother maintained her nine o'clock bedtime.

"How is it?"

"Nice. At least, what I've seen so far. It's a little quiet, though." What seemed like a long time ago, she'd cherished her rare moments of quiet. Now they weighed her down like a wet wool coat.

"Quiet is good, Julia."

She laughed. "The kids driving you crazy already?"

"Not at all. Your dad has them with him most of the day. Shelly's showing signs of being a real farmer. Could be we've finally found someone to take over the farm when we retire."

"My Shelly?"

"That's the one."

"We can't possibly be talking about the same girl, the one who would rather stay home from a party than be caught wearing the wrong jeans."

"I don't know what brand she's got on right now, but she didn't appear to mind wearing them to shovel the manure out of the barn."

Julia felt a guilty surge of pleasure at the news. There was no way Shelly would last the entire summer doing those kinds of chores. She'd be on her way home the minute she thought she could get away with it.

"How is Jason?"

"Limping. I told him how you broke both your legs jumping out of the hayloft that summer you were seventeen and he thought he'd give it a try. I don't know why everyone thinks kids are so different nowadays."

"He's okay?"

"If you could bottle embarrassed and sell it for a dime a jar, he'd be going home rich."

"Is he around? I'd like to get my two cents in."

"He's off fishing with your dad. They left before sunup. They swore they'd bring back enough bluegill for supper, but I took a chicken out of the freezer, just in case."

Her father had been promising Jason he'd take him fishing for years. "Tell them I'll call back tonight."

"Better make it early. They're going into town with Fred to have dinner and see some new vampire movie. He promised it was funny and wouldn't give Jason nightmares."

"How long has Fred been there?" Last she'd heard he was spending the summer on some archeological dig in Utah.

"When he found out the kids were going to be here, he canceled his trip."

"Oh, great." Her slim chance of getting the kids home early had just dropped to none.

"What's wrong?"

"Nothing."

"Did I mention how good it is for your father to have the kids here? Every night he tells me how much they remind him of Evan."

It was her mother's gentle way of saying that while it might seem that she and her father were moving on with their lives, they hadn't forgotten. "Tell them to have a good time at the movie and that I'll catch them tomorrow."

"Take care of yourself, Julia."

"I love you, Mom."

"I love you, too, sweetheart."

David cleaned the trout, put it in the refrigerator for that night's dinner and began his morning routine—an hour going over the pages he'd written the day before in an attempt to breathe life into them with revisions. At the end of the hour, he would give up, delete everything and begin the three hours he spent at the typewriter each day creating the prose that would end up deleted the next day. Only twice since he'd been there had he kept any of his work longer than twenty-four hours.

His agent insisted it wasn't David's talent that had dried up; it was his ability to judge his own work. But he was the only one he cared about pleasing, and in his mind he hadn't written anything worth publishing in four years.

Today it was more than the usual fear and frustration that kept him from sitting at his desk and starting work that used to come as easily as breathing. When Mary Stephens made her monthly call to find out how things were going and see if he needed anything, she'd told him about the recently widowed woman who would be staying at the main house for the summer and asked if he would mind seeing that she got settled in okay. *Widow* implied a stereotype that Julia McDonald didn't fit. He'd expected someone older, someone content to sit on the porch or watch talk shows on the satellite television in the afternoons, someone with enough life experiences to actually want her privacy, too.

Instead, this wounded creature had arrived, still young and vibrant and undoubtedly aching to be a part of life again—not a combination for a woman content to keep her own company.

Even recognizing the unfairness of his assumptions, David let them color his impressions. No wonder he'd slipped into this abyss of depression. Where was the man who'd eagerly sought out people, the one who got up in the morning knowing, without question, that something new, *someone* new, would cross his path that day and his life would be richer for it?

He'd found the caretaker's job through friends, the couple who'd hired him, Harold and Mary Stephens, unaware they were hiring a man to do menial chores whose wealth matched their own. He'd hoped the isolation would either rekindle the fire that once had fueled his passion to write or let him walk away.

What he'd learned was that his anger at injustice still burned as hot, but without the naiveté of youth to sustain the belief that anger could foster change, he had no words.

He sat down at his desk, just him, a mug of coffee and his temperamental laptop…and thoughts of a beautiful and sad woman who'd appeared in his life unbidden and unwelcome.

Two more months and his self-imposed exile would be over. In a way the prospect intrigued him. Not since his years on the road had he felt the heady freedom that came with being unaccountable to anyone or anything.

Perhaps he should thank Julia McDonald for hurrying the process along. She certainly didn't deserve the misdirected hostility that had made him unfit to be around anyone, friend or stranger, for the past three years. He vowed to maintain his distance from her, considering it an act of kindness.

*Six Months Missing*

*Everything I knew about sex I'd learned from books and farm animals and movies and television. Oh, and then there were several girlfriends who were curious or had the lethal combination of persuasive boyfriends and too much to drink and thought keeping a secret meant telling no more than five of your best friends.*

*After all the war stories, I was determined my first time would be cold sober, my choosing and with someone I loved. I must have sent out an invisible do-not-touch signal, because with the kind of boys who did ask me out, it was never a major problem. I'd never been outside my own house completely naked. Except, of course, showers after gym and changing into my swimming suit at the municipal swimming pool. Oh, and at the doctor's office. I even skinny-dipped in my underpants and bra. Given the opportunity to go to a topless beach, I would have been easy to spot—the one with the top on. But then, I digress.*

*Which, I guess, was why I was so surprised that being naked with you that first time seemed so right. I'd left one world, the touch-me-and-you-die one, at the top of the slide and landed in a heap, full force, in another at the bottom. The two of us moved around on my grandmother's pinwheel patchwork quilt in a tangle of arms and legs, sighs and laughter, discovery and passion. I never once hesitated or thought to cover up.*

*For two virgins we did okay. No, it was a whole lot better than okay. I don't know if you innately understood where to touch me or if you picked up on my reactions as you explored my body with those exquisitely gentle hands, but by the time you finally slipped your body between my legs, and after I felt a quick moment of pain, I was on a wondrous journey I hadn't come close to imagining. I was breathless, caught up in a whirlwind and just plain dumbfounded at the intensity of my reaction. I thought I would go crazy with desire.*

*This was a good thing. A really, really good thing. I wanted to do it again. I wanted to do it all the time.*

*You rolled over on your back and grinned at me. I rolled to my stomach, propped myself up on my elbows and returned your smile.*

*"I can see why my dad asked us to wait. I can't imagine studying when we could have been doing this."*

*You laughed. "I take it that means you liked it?"*

*I plucked a piece of grass and lightly ran the tip down your side. "Can we do it again?"*

*"When did you have in mind? Remember, I'm leaving tomorrow morning. Early."*

*"Now?"*

*You shook you head. "Uh-uh."*

*"Why not?"*

*You held up the empty condom wrapper.*

*"It's only good for one time?" If I'd known, I would have taken Fred's entire stash. "So now what?"*

*You put your hand at the back of my neck and brought me to you for a kiss. "Now we lie here in the sun and listen to the birds and eat the lunch you packed and—"*

*How could you talk about listening to some stupid bird when all I could think about was your lips on my breast and your body between my legs? "I guess that means it wasn't as good for you as it was for me?"*

*"Why do you say that?"*

*"You're so…so…casual about it." Today was the most important day of my life. Nothing before had even come close. And here you were cloud-gazing like it was any old day.*

*"I'm sorry. It's just the way I am, Julia."*

*I threw the grass at you. "You could at least tell me you liked it."*

*I know that I'd given as good as I got and I wanted you to be as eager for it to happen again as I was. But maybe most of all I wanted to know that while you were in Detroit you would remember me with the same longing that I had for you. I didn't know until that moment how afraid I was that you would go home and find someone you liked better.*

*How could I compete with sophisticated city girls? Everything I knew about the world outside Kansas I'd learned from magazines.*

*You didn't say anything for a long time and somehow I managed not to jump in with inane chatter to fill the silence. I could see that I'd dampened the joy that you'd been experiencing only moments before and didn't understand what was happening. Had it been awful for you and you were afraid to tell me?*

*"You have to realize that sex isn't the mystery for me that it is for you, Julia."*

*You confused me with that. "Are you saying I'm not—"*

*"My mother was a prostitute."*

*You said it with such acceptance that it almost seemed you were talking about the plot of some R-rated movie. In my world bad mothers were women who fed their kids a steady diet of fast food. I couldn't conceive what it must have been like for you growing up with a woman who earned the rent money selling her body.*

*"Always?" I asked, seeking a good memory.*

*"Yeah—always. When she brought her Johns to the apartment, I'd be sent to the corner market to buy cigarettes, or if she didn't have the money for cigarettes, I'd be shoved out the door to stand in the hallway until she was finished. That's when she re-*

*membered I was even there, which was only about half the time."*

*"How old were you?"*

*You sent me a penetrating stare. "This was how I lived. All my life. I've never associated sex with love or tenderness or caring, only money."*

*"Not even now?" I said, my heart in my throat.*

*"I'm learning. But it's been hard. You want me in a way that has nothing to do with people using each other. I don't understand that. And I don't trust it. Not completely. Not yet."*

*"What can I do to help you?" I had a project. I would find a way for you to see the good in people. In me. I would do whatever I could to give you the joy and trust and love you'd never had.*

*You ignored my question.*

*"I've never seen a man look at a woman the way your dad looks at your mom," you said. "And your mom looks back at him like he's the most handsome, sexiest, funniest guy on earth. Robert Redford could be standing next to Clyde and your mom wouldn't see him." You plucked off the grass that I'd thrown at you and tossed it aside.*

*"The idea of loving someone like that is as foreign to me as palm trees and white sandy beaches. I know they exist, I want to experience them, but I don't have what it takes to believe I'll ever feel that sand between my toes. I want us to*

*have what your mom and dad have, Julia. I want it so much it hurts."*

*"My mom and dad really look at each other like that?" Not that I'd ever seen.*

*"All the time. You don't see it because you don't want to, or maybe you're blind to it because they're your parents."*

*Back then I didn't know how to respond to you when you said something like that. I was too young, my life before you too sheltered, to really understand what you were saying. "You mean they look at each other like this?" I put everything I had into the look I gave you, batting my eyelashes and grinning seductively.*

*You laughed, but I saw a wariness, as if you were thinking it had been a mistake to talk to me about your mother. "Yeah, just like that."*

*"I love you, Evan McDonald." There it was. The fit as natural and right as a fox wearing its own fur. "And I'm going to love you when I'm fifty years old exactly the way I love you now." At the time fifty was as old as I could imagine and the same as saying forever. "If you let me."*

*"What's that supposed to mean?"*

*"If you don't find someone else when you go home."*

*You moved toward me so that we were nearly nose to nose. "What are you talking about?"*

*You really had no idea. "Detroit."*

*"Detroit isn't my home anymore. It's just another city. My home is here. With you. For the rest of my life, wherever you are is where I want to be. How could you not know that?"*

*It wasn't the I love you, too, that I'd been looking for. It was a whole lot better.*

# CHAPTER 8

David put in his three hours at the typewriter, ate his first meal of the day—a bowl of stale cereal—grabbed his tool belt and headed back to the dock to fix the loose board he'd found that morning.

He liked repair work but found more satisfaction in creating the small, one-of-a-kind chests and boxes he made when he needed something to do that had nothing to do with writing. He created his boxes out of layers of contrasting woods glued together in varying patterns, experimenting with color and texture and grain. The finish received as much attention as the construction, and when he was satisfied he'd reached his self-imposed standard of perfection, he gave the box away.

Of the dozens of boxes he'd made, he'd kept only one. Crude in comparison to the others, the wood ordinary white pine, the hinges scavenged from a bin in an old-fashioned hardware store in Enid, Oklahoma. For the past dozen and a half years it had been the depository of the one or two invariable bad reviews that accompanied the publication of his books. They were the only ones he kept, ignoring the ones that proclaimed him a genius and the conscience of the hedonistic eighties and self-indulgent nineties. He used them as reminders of the futility of writing for anything but his own approval.

He saw Julia standing on the dock as soon as he rounded the final turn on the path. She had her back to him, and for an instant he thought about retracing his steps and returning when she'd left. Not until that moment did he realize that his months of solitude had left him with a proprietary feeling about the place. He didn't like knowing that he was no longer there alone, free to come and go without conscious thought or consideration of another person.

He stopped to watch her. By anyone's definition she was a classic beauty. She had the features idealized in marble thousands of years ago by sculptors in love with perfection. She was thinner than the Greek and Roman ideal, her hair shorter, the sadness in her eyes something not even the most skilled artisan could capture in stone.

Despite being annoyed that she was there, David felt a completely unexpected attraction. Obviously, he'd been alone too long. He needed to stop trying to find himself, and get back into the world. The simple fact that he could be attracted to a woman who'd come there to mourn her husband was insane.

She heard his approach and jumped, a fleeting look of panic crossing her eyes. An embarrassed smile followed. "I keep expecting a bear to wander out of the woods."

"I think the hunters cleared them out of this area a long time ago. At least, I haven't seen any while I've been here." David stopped at the end of the dock and put one hand on the waist-high piling, the other on his hip. "I noticed a board coming up this morning and figured I'd better fix it before one of us tripped and took a header into the lake."

"I already fixed it," she said. When he didn't say anything, she added, "I found some tools in the garage. I hope it's okay that I borrowed them."

"Of course it's okay." He shrugged. "Just not expected."

"What? That I can pound a couple of nails? I can fix leaky toilets, too, and cranky sprinkler systems, and wobbling ceiling fans, and you should see what I can do with creaky floor boards." She softened the words with a smile.

"I didn't mean I thought you were incapable, just that I was surprised you'd want to. I was told you were here on vacation." She appeared fresh from a shower, her dark hair damp and curling in a loose cap around her face. Dressed in red shirt, tied at her waist, and white shorts that showed off lean, muscular legs, she seemed a different woman from the one he'd met that morning, younger and somehow less guarded.

"It's been a long time between vacations. Obviously I don't know how to relax anymore."

He shifted his hand to the hammer in his tool belt. "Give it a couple of days. This place will either impose its pace or drive you back to the city."

"What do you do around here? For entertainment, I mean. Is there a theater in town?"

"You'd have to go into Redding for that."

"A video store?"

"The grocery store carries twenty-five or thirty titles, but any that aren't ten years old are gone by noon."

"Sounds like I should find a bookstore."

He hesitated. "I've got a couple of boxes of books I'm donating to the library. You can go through and pick what you want." To make sure she didn't misinterpret his offer as an invitation to visit, he added, "I'll bring them by later and leave them on the porch."

"Thanks."

"Well, I guess I'd better get back."

She shoved her hands in her pockets. "Yeah, me, too."

He caught a movement out of the corner of his eye at the edge of the clearing and turned to see what it was. A flash of white moved between two Douglas firs and then cautiously appeared next to a low-growing gooseberry bush. It was the dog he'd been feeding for several weeks and had named Pearl for her thick, almost iridescent white coat.

Where she'd appeared reasonably healthy before, she now looked emaciated and desperate.

*"Shit,"* David muttered.

"What's wrong?" Julia followed his gaze.

"She's had pups." He should have known she wasn't plump because she was healthy. How could he have been so stupid?

"Who—" But then she saw what David saw. "Oh, my God. She's so skinny."

"She's been gone almost a week. I figured the coyotes had finally gotten her."

"She's *yours?*"

"She's a stray. Or more likely, she was dumped. That happens a lot around here. Whoever had her probably discovered she was pregnant and didn't want to deal with it. I haven't been able to get close enough to see if she has tags."

"She looks like she's starving."

"I'm amazed she's still alive. I've been leaving food

out for her, but plainly not enough. I just assumed she was also getting fed somewhere else. I had no idea she was pregnant."

"What have you been giving her?"

"Whatever I had around the house."

"I'm going to see what I have," Julia said. "Keep an eye on her for me, please."

"She's not going anywhere." David took off his tool belt and laid it on the ground. Pearl watched his every movement.

Within minutes Julia was back, a stack of sandwiches on a plate. David held up his hand when she moved his way. Maybe it was men Pearl feared. "She doesn't trust me. Why don't you try."

Julia nodded. She slowly started across the clearing.

"Talk to her," David said. "Tell her that she's a good dog—and that she's beautiful." They were the words he'd used to gain the little trust Pearl had allowed him.

Snatches of Julia's coaxing drifted to him, things about babies and being a mother mixed with the words *good* and *beautiful*. She was within twenty yards when she stopped, held out one of the sandwiches and then gave it a small toss forward. Julia then backtracked about ten feet and lowered herself to her haunches, purposely looking to the side and not directly at Pearl.

David kept his gaze locked on Pearl, ready to move should she misinterpret Julia's retreat and in her desperation become aggressive. Instead, a wave of pity shot through him so strong it became impossible to remain a bystander in Pearl's life. She trembled as she left the safety of the forest and neared the sandwich, almost falling when she lowered her head to snatch it. Two bites and it was gone. She lifted her head to look at Julia, then at David.

Julia placed the plate on the ground, stood and backed away.

"It's okay," he mouthed, sending words of encouragement to Pearl that she couldn't possibly hear or understand. "Go for it."

Julia walked toward David. "Is she eating?"

"If she doesn't slow down, I'm afraid it's going to come back up."

Not until Julia was beside him did she chance looking at Pearl again, catching one final glimpse as she picked up the last sandwich and carried it into the woods.

"She's not going to make it if we don't do something to help her," Julia said.

"What was in the sandwich?"

"Peanut butter. It was the only protein I had."

He would never have thought to give a dog peanut butter. "I'm surprised she got it down."

"I put butter on the bread first."

"Well, it must have worked." David bent to retrieve his tool belt. "I'll go into town to get some dog food."

"I can get it. I was going anyway."

He nodded.

"Unless you want to go," she said. "She is your dog, after all—well, kind of." When he didn't immediately answer, she said, "Or we could go together."

Oh, hell. This was becoming way too complicated. His life was screwed up enough already without adding a homeless dog and emotionally lost widow. "Be ready in five minutes," he snapped. "I'll pick you up by the garage."

Seeing her justified confusion, he added, "If that's okay with you."

"I'll be there." Her reply lacked her earlier enthusiasm.

David pulled up in a truck that would have been left on the back forty to go to rust in Kansas, leaned across the seat and opened the door. Julia didn't say anything as she climbed in beside him.

"I owe you an apology," he said, grinding the transmission into first gear. "I wasn't expecting company this summer, and like all true curmudgeons I'm a little slow accepting change. I'm sorry if I've come across as less than welcoming."

*Company?* It was a term she would expect from the owner, not the caretaker. "I'll try to stay out of your way from now on."

"That's fair. And I'll do what I can to stay out of yours."

"Now that we have that settled, I was thinking that we can make this trip a lot shorter and get out of each other's way sooner if we stop at the vet's first." She went on to explain that they could buy a specialized food there and she would go back into town to do her grocery shopping another time. Alone.

The vet listened and nodded as David and Julia told him about Pearl. Plainly, it was a story he'd heard before. He wasn't encouraging about their chances of saving her but suggested vitamins and a prescription food for lactating dogs that he thought would give her the best chance.

"You could try to find the puppies before the coyotes do," he said, walking with them through the waiting room. "Provided they're more than a couple of weeks old, you might be able to save one or two of them if the mom doesn't make it."

When they were in the truck again and headed home, Julia said, "I hesitate asking this, considering we just said we would stay out of each other's way, but would you like help looking for Pearl's puppies?"

"I'm not going to try."

Could she have been that wrong about the kind of man he was? "But if we don't—"

"If I follow Pearl, she'll lose the little trust she has in me. When that happens she'll stop coming in for food and then she'll die. If she dies, so do the puppies."

Julia wasn't about to surrender that easily. "There has to be a better answer."

He stiff-armed the steering wheel. "I don't subscribe to lost causes. And as I see it, Pearl isn't a 'we' project. Either I take her on or you do."

So, it was her he didn't like interfering in his life, not Pearl or her puppies. Had she done something to offend him? After years of forcing her way into offices of people working just as hard to keep her out, she truly wasn't aware anymore when she was being pushy or too assertive or simply expressing interest. She wasn't the same woman she'd been before the kidnapping and had no idea how to go back. Or if she even wanted to.

"I'm sorry. I'll butt out." She rolled down the window, let the wind whip her hair and stared at the passing trees. "Pearl is all yours."

They were almost to the house when David said, "No, I'm sorry. I've been acting like a jerk." He took in a deep breath. "Let's work on getting her back to my place with food and then we'll station ourselves at points along her route to see if we can figure out where she's hidden her puppies."

She could hear the doubt in his voice; he didn't believe for a minute that it would work. But she was grateful he was willing to make the attempt, and that he had included her in the effort. She would have a hard time getting through the day knowing someone or something needed her and she wasn't doing everything she could.

"Thank you," she told him.

He rewarded her one of his heart-stopping smiles. "You're welcome." After several seconds, he added, "I'm sorry about today. Can we begin again?"

She'd known few men in her life who apologized—at least, few whom she believed. For most, the words were a means to an end. She decided right then, without reservation and despite their rocky start, that she liked David Prescott.

She returned his smile. "Consider it done."

That night when Julia called Shelly and Jason, she told them about Pearl, grateful to have something to talk about other than how much she missed them.

"Grandma's cat had kittens," Shelly said cautiously after they'd exhausted the discussion about Pearl.

Her mother was a founding member of the Bickford Animal Shelter and fanatical about spaying and neutering. It was highly unlikely that she'd allowed one of her cats to get pregnant. "Grandma's cat?" Julia questioned.

"Well, not exactly. It's one she brought home from the shelter. The mom is almost a kitten herself and Grandma didn't think she would know what to do when she had her own babies. They're so-o-o-o-o cute, Mom." She rushed on before Julia could say anything. "She said I could have one—if it's okay with you. Is it? I really, really want this gray-and-white one. He's been sleeping with me and he follows me everywhere. Grandma said she would pay for his shots and that she'd have him fixed as soon as he's old enough so you wouldn't have to do anything when he comes home."

It was on the tip of Julia's tongue to ask what would happen to the cute little kitten that would become a full-grown cat by the time Shelly left for college, but she'd been the bearer of negative answers for so long that she leaped at the opportunity to be positive. "Okay."

Shelly shrieked. "Thank you, Mom. Thank you, thank you, thank you. You won't be sorry. I promise. I'll do everything. You'll never have to feed him or change the litter box or anything."

Julia believed that the way she believed she would be the million-dollar grand-prize winner if she bought a magazine subscription. "Have you named him?"

"Grandma told me not to, but I did anyway. I'm calling him Orlando."

Julia didn't have to ask why. Shelly, like half her friends, had a bedroom wall covered in Orlando Bloom posters. "I like it."

"I suppose I should tell you that Jason will probably want one, too. There's this scrawny little black one that the mom rejected that Grandma has been helping Jason bottle-feed."

How could she tell Jason no when she'd told Shelly yes? Maybe Shelly was wrong and Jason wouldn't ask.

"Jason wants to talk to you, Mom," Shelly said.

So much for that idea.

*Six Months and a Day Missing*

*"I'm pregnant," I blurted out. It wasn't anything like the way I'd planned to tell you. I'd spent the day going over how to lead you into the news gently. The timing was terrible. We were in the middle of junior-year finals and you were a week away from your last summer in Detroit. I held my breath and waited.*

*You went from wide-eyed surprise to full-face grin, picked me up and swung me around, which was an amazing feat in our tiny apartment, and plopped down on the couch with me in your lap. "When did you find out?"*

*"You're not upset?"*

*"Hell, no. Why would I be?"*

*Perversely, your enthusiasm rattled me, even made me a little angry. I'd prepared arguments to convince you that having a baby wasn't the disaster it seemed, and you were over-the-moon happy. "Oh, I don't know. How about we still have a year before we graduate, we're not married, you're about to leave for three months, we're—"*

*"Two-and-a-half months."*

*"What?" I glared at you. "I'm telling you my life is in shambles and all you can do is correct my time line? Are you crazy?" You caught me as I moved to get up and pulled me back down.*

*"We can do this, Julia." You kissed me then—*

*a kiss filled with such warmth and longing and passion that my unreasoning fury melted like a marshmallow in a campfire.*

*"How?" I asked, so near to tears my chin quivered.*

*"We'll work on that later," you said. "Right now I want to celebrate. With you—"You put your hand on my still-flat belly. "And with our baby."*

*We dug through the couch and chairs and under the seats in the car and in the ashtray and came up with two dollars and twenty-three cents. The side pocket of my purse yielded a five-dollar bill, which to us at the time was tantamount to finding a fortune. You took the bottles we'd been collecting back to the store, added it to the change we'd found and came home with an incredible feast. That night we spread a blanket out in a wheat field and ate brie and crackers and grapes and toasted our lives together with sparkling cider. We made love for the first time without any protection. It was so-o-o-o unbelievably sexy to have that kind of freedom that I swore we'd never go back to condoms, which plainly couldn't be counted on anyway. When we'd exhausted positions and each other, we lay with arms and legs entangled and counted stars.*

*You pointed out the Big Dipper and said, "See the second star on the handle?"*

*I nodded, my chin rhythmically bumping your shoulder.*

*"That's our star from now on."*

*"Why that one?"*

*"It's not one—it's four. They're so near each other, astronomically speaking, that they look like one."*

*I'd learned by then to stop questioning how you knew these kinds of things. You absorbed and stored knowledge like an intellectual sponge. "And you chose this star—"*

*"Mizar."*

*"You chose Mizar because?"*

*"It represents our family. Or the family we will have one day."*

*"We haven't had our first baby and you're already planning a second?"*

*"Two against two. Us against them. It's only fair to even the odds, don't you think?"*

*I'd thought about having a family with you, of course, but not this soon. We had another year of school ahead of us and then graduation, jobs to find, moving and settling into a new apartment. Adding a baby to the mix complicated everything. How was I going to fit labor and delivery around finals? I couldn't possibly care for a brand-new baby and go to classes. I was going to have to quit school, at least for a semester. I started hyperventilating.*

*"Hey," you said, and drew me closer. "I didn't mean to scare you. If you really don't want two, we don't have to—"*

*"I don't know how I'm going to deal with one," I admitted. "I can't think about two. Not yet. Maybe not ever." What I was trying to tell you was that I was scared. Really scared. I still hadn't become a wife and I was going to be a mother.*

*The wife part was settled when we eloped without telling anyone. We expected my mom and dad to be hurt, but being able to add that we were married when they announced they were becoming grandparents went a long way in salving the wounds. As always, they pitched in and loaded us up with everything we could possibly need for a new baby, including giving us their time whenever possible.*

*That was the last summer I spent on the farm. My mother realized I would only be back for visits from then on and spent the entire time adjusting her moods to accommodate joy at having her married and pregnant daughter under her wing and sorrow knowing it would never happen again.*

*You and I did fine. No, we did better than fine. When Shelly was born in January, you took to being a father as if you'd been programmed for the job. I used to imagine you with your baby brother and liked knowing that he'd had you to love and care for him during his short life.*

*I didn't have to drop out of school, even though we spent the first six months of Shelly's life like loving zombies. We were lucky to share a kiss as we passed each other on our way to and from class and to and from doing the baby duty. Sleep turned into a distant memory; sex, too.*

*And then it all came together—graduation, job offers, and a baby who not only slept through the night but also slept in on weekends and gave us time to rediscover each other in some really fun ways.*

*The hard part was after the party my folks threw to celebrate all the changes in our lives and we had to tell them that you'd accepted a job—in California. Mom cried; Dad dug deep and came up with a smile.*

*If he'd been aware we were starting a Warren family exodus to the West Coast, he might not have been so gracious.*

# CHAPTER 9

For two days Julia and David got up at dawn and planted themselves along the path they'd seen Pearl take into the forest. Julia was surprised at how comfortable she felt with David as they sat without talking and how often she noted they were drawn to the same things in their silent, sheltered environment. He pointed out a pileated woodpecker's nest in the cavity of a dead tree and Julia reciprocated when she discovered a tiny lichen-covered cup held together with spider webs. Nestled inside were two almost impossibly small rufous hummingbird babies.

Julia decided that it wasn't all that unusual to feel comfortable with someone in conversation, but it was rare to feel such ease in sitting together in silence, especially with a man who was basically a stranger to her.

The only times they saw Pearl was when she appeared, like an apparition, beside the tree where they'd left her food.

Missing her again that third morning, they figured she wouldn't be back for a couple of hours and that they might as well get on with their day. Julia was halfway across the pine-needle-covered open area that passed for David's front yard when he called to her. "Would you like a cup of coffee?"

When she'd made the same offer to him the day before, he'd declined and then quickly explained that his mornings were taken. If he didn't work then, he didn't work at all. "But I thought—"

"I'm taking a day off," he said.

"Then, sure. I'd love a cup." Thank God for coffee, the great socializer.

"Come on in. It will only take a minute." He paused before going inside. "Or you could wait out here on the porch. Whatever makes you more comfortable."

What was with David? She'd never met anyone more push-pull. "I'll come in, if that's okay. I need to use the bathroom."

He held the door. "It's in the back, down the hall to your right."

As she made her way through the house, she subconsciously noted how he lived—what was important enough to keep, how often he cleared the coffee table of cups and cans and what reading material he had lying around. Paying attention to those kinds of details was a girl thing, readily understood by her girlfriends but never by any guy she'd known. Not even Evan. He thought what she and her girlfriends did was snooping, pure and simple. Every female she knew applied a different, kinder, word—*curiosity*.

What she found wasn't anything like she'd imagined. She'd assumed that David's "work" had something to do with fixing things around the property. But the prominence of a desk and computer and peripheral material in the living room made it plain that whatever he was doing away from the daily upkeep of the property wasn't physical. She glanced at the books on the desk. They were mostly volumes of poetry and essays and biographies. She stopped to look at the one lying open.

"Walt Whitman," David said from the kitchen doorway. *"Leaves of Grass."*

"A favorite collection of yours?"

"For several reasons."

"My father is always quoting Whitman. 'Crossing Brooklyn Ferry' in particular."

He nodded. "It's in there."

"Is there one you like to quote, too?" she asked, sensing his answer would tell her more than he would reveal by direct questioning. *Now watch him pick a poem she didn't know.*

"I never quote poetry," he said. And then, as if realizing how dismissive he sounded, he added, "But lines from 'I Sit and Look Out' run through my head whenever I read a newspaper or watch the news on television. I think of them as my conscience."

She didn't recall the entire poem, but the last line came to her complete, one of the bizarre bits of trivia that cluttered her mind and took over space where more important things should reside. "'All these—All the meanness and agony without end, I sitting, look out upon. See, hear, and am silent.'" Realizing what she'd done, she laughed. "Obviously, I fall into the quoting category."

"I won't hold it against you."

"Thanks. I promise it won't happen again." A promise embarrassingly easy to keep. Until that line popped out of her mouth, she would have sworn she'd never memorized any lines of poetry. "Are you a writer?" she guessed.

"I used to be. Whatever kept me going in the beginning seems to have disappeared, however."

"Published?"

"Some."

The "used to be" didn't make sense with the desk and computer. And once you had one book published, wasn't that all you needed to guarantee others would follow? "Should I have heard of you?"

"Not necessarily. It depends on what you like to read."

"At one time I read just about everything," she said. "I was hoping to get back to it while I'm here."

He pointed to several boxes of books. "Like I said, you're welcome to whatever interests you."

"Do you have anything of yours?"

He shook his head. "Unless you read Spanish. I had some foreign-language copies of one of my books arrive the other day that I was going to give to the library."

"As a matter of fact, I do."

He hesitated and then shrugged. "I'll dig one out after we've had our coffee."

She left for the bathroom then because it would have seemed strange not to. She even succeeded in not peeking inside the medicine cabinet. That really would have crossed the line into snooping. She did, however, glance around again as she walked back through the living room.

A thin layer of dust coated most surfaces, but she'd already discovered that was a given with the wood-burning stoves both houses used for heat at night. A red plaid pillow sitting propped against the arm of the sofa told her David liked to lie down when he read. Judging by the deep indentation in the pillow, he read a lot. There were books stacked three and four deep sitting on most flat surfaces, the only real clutter in the room. His desk held his laptop and books and little else.

"Coffee's ready," David called.

She joined him in the kitchen. "Why don't we drink it on the porch. Maybe we'll get lucky and Pearl will stop by."

David handed her a mug and held the door. They settled into creaking wicker rocking chairs, sinking into faded blue-and-white striped cushions.

"Did you hear the coyote the other night?" she asked. "He sounded so close, almost as if he were standing in the middle of the front yard."

David had, but wasn't going to mention it. The excited barking was something coyotes did when protecting a kill. The longer they'd gone without seeing Pearl, the more worried he had become. "Without any traffic noise to mute it, sound travels a long way here."

She seemed satisfied with the answer.

"The view from your place is completely different from mine," she said, plainly struggling for conversation. "It's almost as if I'm looking at a different lake."

He hid his smile. They'd known each other almost a week, long enough that they were past the initial awkwardness of strangers but not long enough for anything personal, especially after their shaky start. But the more he was around her, the more he found to like and the less inclined he was to fight the attraction. She was smart and direct and had a sexiness that emanated from her like light from a campfire at midnight.

He looked out at the small cove and island that were hidden from her place by the stand of trees that separated them. "I think in this case the caretaker's cottage has the real money view."

A pair of geese swam by. They should have been in Alaska months ago, but David had learned from a couple who lived on the other side of the lake that this pair remained year-round. Every winter they lost their young to the flocks of migrating geese that stopped to rest before flying farther south, the call of the wild stronger than the plaintive cry of the parents.

"Did you know they mate for life, just like swans?" Julia said. "I've never heard what happens when one of them dies." She watched the gander circle and head toward shore. The goose followed. "Do you suppose the one left behind eventually gives up and dies, too?"

The question carried deeper meaning. He didn't have to hear Julia's story to see that she was still hurting. "People die of broken hearts all the time. I don't know why the same thing couldn't happen to birds."

"That's something Evan might have said. He believed most of us are too egocentric to acknowledge we aren't the only sentient creatures on earth."

"He sounds like a man I would have liked. What happened to him?" The invitation to cross the barrier that had separated them until now surprised them both a little.

"He died. Six months—" She covered the awkward moment by taking a sip of coffee. "Actually, he died five and a half years ago."

"Too strong?" David asked, noting the face she'd made and supplying her an opportunity to change the subject.

"Hotter than I expected."

"There's ice in the freezer."

"It's fine."

Before he could say anything more, she picked up where she'd left off. "Evan has been dead five and a half years, but I only found out six months ago."

He didn't say anything, waiting for her to continue or not. The story was hers to tell. The geese came onshore to nibble the short grass by the edge of the lake. Seconds stretched into minutes. Julia took another sip of coffee and then another. Finally, the coffee gone, she began.

When she finished filling David in on her life for the past six years, giving him a highly abbreviated version, she said, "As you've undoubtedly figured out, I'm having trouble letting go."

"I can understand that." For most, the kind of love she had had with Evan only happened in books and movies. David had known a lot of women, had even loved a couple of them, or at least had felt something he'd thought was love. But when the relationship had ended, he'd always been able to walk away without looking back.

"On some level my friends and family recognize that what Evan and I had was special, but now that he's gone, they're eager for me to get past losing him. No one understands what we had was a lifetime thing. For me, there is no moving on."

They were simple words, spoken in a matter-of-fact manner and heartbreaking in their finality. Julia frowned. "Somehow, everyone I know seems to have found a way to accept that Evan has been gone five and a half years, while for me... I still can't believe he's gone."

"It's probably because he was more real to you during the time he was missing than he was to them." That was as deep as he wanted to get into suggesting answers for something so personal.

"It won't matter how much time passes. I'm never going to feel any different. I will always be connected to Evan the way I am now." She blinked, as if abruptly waking. "I'm sorry. I don't know why I told you that. I don't usually—"

"It's okay. I like listening to you. Passionate people intrigue me." He was drawn by the depth of her feelings, and wondered what it would be like to love and be loved by someone the way Julia loved David. With a bittersweet sadness he knew it was a world he would never inhabit.

An embarrassed smile tugged at one corner of her mouth. "Me and Whitman?"

"I'd like to think there might be one or two more of your type out there."

"Like you?"

David didn't answer right away. He never shared his feelings outside his books. It was something both the women he'd lived with and said that he loved had complained about, and in the end told him was a reason for leaving. "I feel things deeply," he admitted. "But they are never as benign as love. Anger fuels my passions."

"Could that be why you're having trouble writing? You've mellowed?"

He laughed at that. "In my mind I can stand on a soapbox with the best of the sixties radicals. But like most of them, I eventually stopped believing raging at injustice can make a difference."

"I understand." Julia tucked her feet under her and settled deeper into the chair. "Hope died for me, too. It would appear we're climbing the same mountain."

He held up his cup in a salute. "Here's to a fellow climber."

"Mind telling me how you got there?"

He did. Curious reporters had dug around and discovered bits and pieces of his background, but not enough to draw conclusions or come close to figuring him out.

He'd left home at fifteen, abandoning a father who handed out beatings like unshelled peanuts at a road house. Had David stayed, he would either have killed or been killed by his father. His mother had slipped a hundred dollars in his jacket pocket, kissed him goodbye and agreed it was for the best.

Wherever he'd found himself, in whatever circumstances, he'd given an honest day's work when he needed food or money, but never stuck around for two. He slept in forests and doorways, wearing out almost as many sleeping bags as jeans, living off the land when possible and off the kindness of strangers when not. He'd been confronted by cops on six continents, witnessed a man die trying to outrun an angry mob and lent brawn to the rescue of a wild elephant by African villagers whose crops would have been better off if the animal had died. He'd watched the sun set in the Antarctic and rise over the Himalayas and thrown up from seasickness in every major ocean.

David told Julia about his travels but left out the reason he'd gone. "Then I woke up one morning in a hut in South Africa, being eaten alive by some insect I couldn't name, and decided it was time to come home."

A sadness filled Julia's eyes. "When I'm feeling generous, I tell myself it was a good thing that Evan didn't have to put up with the heat and insects and disease in the jungle all those years. But that doesn't happen very often. The selfish part of me would have him put up with anything."

"Third-world countries can get pretty rough for those of us used to four walls and indoor plumbing."

"How old were you when you quit traveling?"

"Twenty. I worked a few odd jobs in South Africa until I found a cargo ship headed the direction I wanted to go, with a captain willing to let me work for my keep." He'd landed in New York with only his journals and a change of clothes and a gnawing hunger for knowledge. Without a high-school diploma and less than fifteen dollars in his pocket, attending college like everyone else was out of the question. Instead, he'd audited classes that interested him, moving from campus to campus to find new voices, new ideas, new perspectives.

"I kept a journal," he said. "I kept dozens, actually. I wrote every day. It was a way for me to vent and not scare the crap out of all the kids around me who thought a crisis was running out of beer money." David laughed. "I was a real firebrand back then, believing one person could effect change. I was convinced all I had to do was discover my voice."

"And did you?" Julia asked.

"In a way. I discovered *Leaves of Grass* and started writing longer and more intensely thought-out pieces." It was at his darkest moment that the essays took over his journals. He experimented with the rhythm and cadence of sentences and paragraphs as if they were weapons, expressing his frustration at the self-absorbed society of the eighties with words written in staccato bursts.

"So, you're a poet?"

He laughed. "Not even close. Today's poets are all songwriters. I could no more do that than I could carry a tune. My writing is all over the place." The bulk of his fame and income had come from the anthologies put together from pieces he'd done for newspapers and magazines.

"I'm impressed."

"Don't be. Opinionated people who think what they say matters to anyone but themselves are as common as allergies nowadays. If you watch Sunday-morning television, it's filled with either self-proclaimed pundits or infomercials."

"So how did you go from journal keeping to published author?"

"A girl I knew had a contact." He'd met Cassidy in Boston during Christmas break. Emancipated by a father no longer willing to support her college habit, she'd waited tables in an Italian restaurant that David had frequented, a place where the pasta was cheap and plentiful. They'd slept together the first night and moved in together the next day. With a background of wealth and privilege, she'd dealt with poverty as if it were a novelty, spending an entire paycheck on a dress that caught her eye in a store window and eating customers' leftovers at the restaurant the rest of the week.

When she discovered David's cache of essays, she automatically assumed he wrote because he wanted to be published. Her family owned a publishing company; she understood how these things worked. Secretly, to surprise him and spare him the pain of possible rejection—or so she told him later—she sent copies of his work to her father.

Not until her father called with an offer did she acknowledge she'd used David's work as a peace offering, seeking a way back into her family's good graces. Poverty's charm had worn thin.

At first David had been furious at what he considered a betrayal and then he'd become pragmatic. He'd never believed poverty had charm. Settling on the anonymity of a pseudonym, he signed a contract and turned his work over to an editor. He and Cassidy parted amicably. She met and married a lawyer and moved into an apartment overlooking Central Park. David bought an old Volkswagen bus and headed west.

A year later, after reading an advance copy of the book, a *New York Times* critic proclaimed "Nicolas Golden" the spokesman of his generation, coining the phrase, "The Man with the Golden Voice."

David hated every part of the sudden and explosive attention that followed. Some saw his refusal to give interviews as a marketing ploy. It wasn't, but it gave the slim book of essays and observations far more press than it would have received had David accepted the dozens and then hundreds of requests for an appearance. The momentum built until *Flying on Clipped Wings* became the book everyone felt the need to own but few actually read or understood.

"That's it?" Julia questioned. "You knew someone who knew someone and you were on your way?"

"Pretty much."

"Was the book successful?"

"More so than it deserved."

"Are you being modest or hypercritical?"

"Neither. As much as we'd all like to think we know what we're talking about when we're in our early twenties, it takes a few more years to gain the experience and maturity to do anything but rant."

"Did you make lots of money?"

He could see that while she was interested in his answers, her questions were directed in ways to keep him talking. She was lonely and afraid he was going to do what he'd done every other day—send her home with the excuse he had work to do. How could she know that she'd been the first thing he'd thought of when he'd woken up that morning, and that he'd lain there for a half hour, trying to figure out why.

What was so special about Julia McDonald that being with her made him think of possibilities over regrets?

"After being in a place where having twenty dollars left after I paid the rent made me rich, I felt like the guy digging a well hoping for water and striking oil," he told her. "I had no idea what to do with that kind of money."

Julia laughed. "I hope you didn't tell people that."

"I did—in an interview I agreed to as a favor to another writer. I was young and dumb, and after the piece hit the stands, I wound up a target for every cause that could locate me. It took a couple of years to sort through who wanted money, who needed it and who deserved it."

"So you just gave it all away?"

"Not all." He still had far more than he could or would ever use.

"Is that why you took the caretaker job—because the writing hasn't been going well?" She made a face. "Ouch. That's a little personal. Sorry."

He could let her believe he needed the money and be done with it. But she was the first person he'd talked to about his writing in years who didn't have a clue who he was, and it felt too good to let go that easily. Once someone realized that his writing had been quoted by presidents and popes, pundits and all manner of idiots, that the thoughts and arguments he'd presented on some obscure radio talk shows were used by politicians on both sides of the aisle to make points he'd never intended, a wall went up. He became Nicolas Golden, someone too important to talk to about life's ordinary vagaries and complaints. In the end he'd ended up so isolated and insulated that the fire in his belly was extinguished by the champagne of his existence.

How should he answer her? He looked at her. Not a glance, but a steady, full-on look. He realized with a start that he cared what she thought. When had this happened? How? More important, why? "I took the job to see if there was anything left of the man I once was. I've been hiding behind distractions for too many years, using them as excuses for work that was mediocre at best. Here it's me and the computer."

"Put up or shut up," she said.

"Succinct but accurate."

"And?"

Yesterday he'd been ready to pack it in. Today something kept him from admitting defeat. At least, out loud. And especially to Julia. "I'm still working on it."

It was her turn to raise her coffee cup in salute. "Here's to both of us finding our way."

David started to return the gesture, when a flash of white caught his eye. "Well, would you look at that," he whispered.

Julia let out a small cry of wonder. Half-hidden

by the trunk of a massive pine, Pearl stared back, a tiny, squirming, black-and-white puppy nestled between her front paws.

*Six Months and Two Days Missing*

*California, land of palm trees, sandy beaches, balmy breezes, the world's finest wines, Yosemite and Disneyland. We'd seen enough ads every winter showing Kansas buried in six-foot snowdrifts and Californians basking in the sun that we never doubted what we would find—beaches connected to spectacular mountains.*

*How could two people who'd graduated college with honors be so dumb? How had we missed questioning what was in that vast Sacramento Valley, which separated the ocean and the mountains? What were we thinking?*

*Whatever it was, reality rolled out a 110-degree welcome mat on that blindingly bright, cloudless Fourth of July day when we dropped out of the Sierra Nevada and into our new home, Sacramento. The city was huge; the surrounding countryside, as flat as home. Traffic was terrifying: mile after mile of race-car drivers merging on and off the freeway, while I sat white knuckled, convinced our Kansas plates made us some kind of target. I was ready to turn around and go home the minute I got out of the car at the service station, accidentally touched the fender and burned myself. I was positive you felt the same way and were somewhere between crying and screaming, but you came back from asking directions, grinning from ear to ear.*

*"The motel is around the corner," you said. "We*

*must have driven right past it." You planted a kiss on my sweaty nose. "And wait until you hear this. All we have to do is stand outside our door tonight and we'll have a front-row seat for a huge fireworks display."*

*I didn't say anything. It wasn't that your enthusiasm was contagious. I just didn't have the heart to stick a pin in your balloon. I figured you had to remove those rose-colored glasses eventually, if only to wipe off the smog.*

*But you didn't. You loved everything about California, and slowly, without being consciously aware of it happening, I did, too. Barbara arrived for a visit and fell in love with the guy in the apartment next door. Mom was beside herself that another daughter was leaving and cried all the way through the wedding. She half-jokingly threatened Fred with bodily harm if he even thought about leaving Kansas. He applied for a job at UCLA the next year.*

*If your job with Stephens Engineering planted our feet in California soil, Jason became the cement that bound us here. Created the night you greeted me in the bedroom wearing nothing but the ridiculous, heart-covered briefs I'd gotten you for Valentine's Day and a rose tucked between your teeth, Jason was the first generation of my family born outside Kansas in a hundred years.*

*My mother couldn't stop crying the day he was born, reinforcing her reputation as the family weeper.*

*She'd tried to talk me into coming "home" for Jason's birth, but I knew how important it was for you to start our own traditions. I managed to resist her, even though it was something I'd secretly wanted, too.*

*You've always been so wonderful with my mother, understanding and funny, calling her without my prompting to include her in the milestones of Shelly's and Jason's lives and sending enough pictures to wallpaper every room in her house. You voluntarily put your dreams of traveling on hold so that we could spend vacations on the farm. I haven't told you often enough how much that meant to me. I'm sorry. I promise I'll tell you every day when you're home again.*

*And I'll tell you that I love you, over and over again, so often that it will echo in your mind when you're sleeping.*

*I do it now.*

*Can you hear me?*

# CHAPTER 10

Silent tears slid down Julia's cheeks when she saw Pearl's torn ear and the blood on her coat. She'd coaxed her into moving closer with food and soft words while David gathered blankets and stuffed them under the porch for a makeshift den. David left a trail of dog treats to entice her toward the house, then stood at a distance to give her time to explore.

"How badly do you think she's hurt?" Julia whispered.

"I'm hoping it's just the ear," David said. "Her throat and belly seem okay—or at least, what I could see of them. Even a coyote would have trouble getting through all that hair on her back."

Pearl gave them a wary glance before she left her puppy on the ground by the steps and crawled under the porch to look around. She stayed long enough that Julia hoped it had won her approval, but just as Julia's hopes rose, Pearl came out and picked up the puppy and turned away. She circled the house, climbed onto the porch and moved inside the house.

Julia looked at David, her mouth open in surprise. "What do you suppose she's doing in there?"

David shoved his hands in his back pockets. "I'm not sure."

They waited...and waited. And waited. Finally, Pearl returned—without her puppy. She headed across the opening and into the forest without a backward glance.

"She must have more puppies," Julia said.

David touched the small of her back and gave her a nudge. "Let's see where she left the first one before she gets back."

They found it in the closet in David's bedroom, curled up on a pile of dirty clothes. Julia looked closer at the plump, squirming ball of black-and-white fur. "It's a girl," she said. "Her eyes are open."

"Then she's more than two weeks old."

"How do you know that?"

"I worked in a shelter for a couple of months when I was in Utah. Most of the puppies' eyes opened sometime between ten and fifteen days."

He moved past her to adjust the clothing into a

flatter, broader surface, giving Pearl more room to lie down when she returned. "She's either decided to trust me or I'm her port in a storm of coyotes."

Pearl was back in less than ten minutes, another puppy in her mouth. Julia saw right away that there was something wrong with this one. The right back leg was stiff and swollen and the puppy was more limp than relaxed in Pearl's mouth.

Julia and David had decided not to wait on the porch, where Pearl would have to walk between them to get into the house. Instead, they sat on chairs in the living room, reminding the dog that she was sharing her den and letting her know that it was safe to be around them.

Pearl stood in the middle of the room, glanced at the doorway into the bedroom and then back again at Julia. She made a muted crying noise before she crossed the room and laid the puppy at Julia's feet. "What do I do now?" Julia asked David.

"Go with your instinct."

Julia peered into Pearl's eyes. She talked to her, soft words of encouragement, words from one mother to another. She put her hand on Pearl's muzzle and then her head, careful not to touch her ear. Instead of picking up the puppy, Julia lowered herself to sit beside it. Unlike its sister, this one didn't respond when she put her hand on its side. "It's a boy," Julia said. "He has a wound on his leg and it appears really nasty."

Pearl nosed the puppy closer to Julia. "I know this sounds crazy, but I think she wants me to help him."

David handed her the fleece blanket draped over the back of the sofa and reached for the phone. "I'll call the vet and tell him we're bringing him in."

"I'll do it," she said. "You stay here so Pearl doesn't think we've conspired to steal her puppy. We don't want her to take off and disappear again. Not now."

Julia wasn't clear of the driveway, before she decided the puppy should have a name. "How does Rufus sound?" she asked him. She waited for a reaction. "No? Then how about Spot for that really cute spot between your eyes?" Again no reaction. This time she put her finger on his side to make sure he was still breathing. She let out a small cry of relief when she felt his tiny chest move up and down. She really, really didn't want him to die. She needed to win this one.

"Okay, so you're not crazy about the standard stuff. How about Francis? That's a good solid name that you don't run into very often. You can bet there won't be a lot of dogs at the dog park turning to look when your person calls that name."

He maneuvered to lift his head. It teetered upright for several seconds before falling to the side. That was indication enough for her. "Okay, Francis it is."

Julia touched his chin. Francis captured her little finger, took it in his mouth and sucked hard. "Good boy," she said, heartened at his strength and the cry of protest that followed when he discovered her finger wasn't what he'd expected. He was stronger than he appeared. "Hang in there, Francis. Help is only a half hour away."

Julia made it in twenty minutes. There were six people in the waiting room. When the frazzled receptionist refused to let her go in first, Julia didn't bother arguing. Instead, she unwrapped Francis and showed him to everyone ahead of her. Five years of dealing with bureaucrats had taught her direct and effective ways to get what she wanted.

The vet, the same one she and David had talked to about Pearl, did a quick assessment and said, "It's a good thing you brought him here right away. This little guy is in pretty bad shape."

"How bad?" Julia asked.

"The leg isn't broken, but he could still lose it if we can't get the infection under control." He continued to manipulate Francis's leg as he talked. "And there's no guarantee that amputation would work. How hard do you want me to try to save him?"

"Can he function with three legs?"

"Very well."

"Then I want you to do whatever it takes." She scooped Francis off the table and into her arms to keep him warm in the overly air-conditioned room. He responded by snuggling against her and nosing the inside of her elbow. She knew she should give him to the vet, but wasn't ready to let go. "What do you think happened to him?"

"It looks like a bite," he said. Then added, "Probably coyote." That confirmed what she and David had already guessed. "She was probably bringing him back to her own pups for lunch. I'm surprised this little guy's mom managed to rescue him."

"I'm going to need something for his mom, too. She has a pretty mangled ear."

"I'm assuming she's the one you were here about last week."

Julia nodded.

"I'll give you an antibiotic that you can put in her food."

The vet took Francis and tucked him under his chin, where he weakly began rooting around again before finally latching onto a piece of soft skin. "Stop worrying. This guy is going to do fine."

Julia took the road back to David's house that circled the lake. It was shorter and more scenic, but took as much time as the direct route because of twists and hairpin turns. She kept glancing at the empty blanket in the front seat next to her surprised at how consumed she was with the need to protect Pearl's puppy.

She rolled the thought over and over in her mind, a sharp rock in a riverbed filled with smooth stones.

Was it the puppy Julia so desperately wanted to protect...or was it Pearl? What would she think when Julia came back empty-handed? Would she be frantic, or would she accept the seeming loss and devote herself completely to the one puppy she had left?

Maybe Julia should stay away until it was time for Francis to come home. That way Pearl wouldn't have to—

What was wrong with her? Why had she stepped so willingly onto this slippery slope of worry? She must be suffering parenting withdrawal, or maybe she'd developed a compulsive impulse to nurture.

Or maybe it was a desire to be nurtured herself. She was worn down from the need to be strong for Shelly and Jason, from pretending she believed she could build a life worth living without Evan and from getting up every morning knowing the fight was over and that she'd lost.

Or maybe it was meeting a man so like Evan they could have been brothers. David was an aching reminder of what she had lost and what she would live without the rest of her life.

She had wonderful friends and the absolute best family. She had children who loved and looked up to her, children she would sacrifice her life to protect. She had to believe that all this, over time, would ease the ache in her heart. To think otherwise was too painful to conceive.

She could tell herself that her life would get better, that time and distance would dull the pain, but it was like all lies, filled with holes and predestined for collapse. Meeting David had brought that home in a way nothing else could. She was lonely beyond imagining.

Abruptly overcome with a powerful longing for a man she hadn't seen in almost six years, a man she would never see again, Julia pulled to the side of the road, let out a strangled cry and covered her face with her hands. She sat behind the wheel, sobbing uncontrollably until she was spent.

Exhausted and reluctant to let David see her with blotchy skin and swollen eyes and face the questions that would undoubtedly follow when he made the obvious assumption something had happened to Pearl's puppy, she got out of the car and walked to the lake. She wandered along the shore until she found a log and sat there to watch trout rise to feed on the afternoon caddis hatch. A piece of bark crumbled beneath her hands, on its way to becoming part of the soil that would feed a new generation of trees.

In death there was life...and heartache...and renewal. It was the natural order of things.

On the island the grass parted and the pair of year-round geese she and David had seen earlier lowered themselves into the water. This time they were accompanied by half a dozen fuzzy yellow goslings. Julia gasped—in surprise and then delight. *Where had they been hiding?*

Had Julia's mother been sitting beside her, she would have insisted the moment was a sign. Or maybe it was a cosmic gift that she'd come here at precisely the right moment to witness something to lessen her pain, and bring a smile.

Julia had no idea how long she sat there and absorbed her tiny miracle, only that after a while, somehow, she seemed less sad.

"Enjoy them while you can," Julia called out as she put her hands on her knees, stood and stretched. Considering what she'd said, she laughed. "Just be careful that you don't turn into clingy, overbearing parents and drive those sweet babies away before their time." She waited another minute for the parade to pass before heading back to the car.

The futility of her sorrow hovered over her like a cloud that refused to drop its rain. If grief were a coin she could spend to change the world, she had enough to stop the famines in Africa and negotiate for peace in the Middle East. But beyond personal pain, it had no value.

She had to find another way to remember Evan. A way he would approve of.

For now, Pearl and her puppies, maybe even David needed her.

Maybe almost as much as she needed them.

*One Year, Five Months, and Four Days missing*

*There's no way for you to know this, Evan, but I haven't written to you for a few months. Actually, it's been almost a year. I had a hard time coming back after we paid the second ransom and then received the letter that said it wasn't enough. I was so sure our ordeal was over at last that I took Shelly and Jason to Bogotá so they could fly home with us, something I swore I'd never do.*

*I've fallen in love with Colombia and the people who've opened their hearts and homes to me. But fear is a constant companion when I'm there. I won't ever expose our children to that kind of danger again.*

*I don't know what to do anymore, Evan. I've begged and pleaded and thrown temper tantrums with every official I can corner both here and at home. They've been incredibly tolerant and understanding, but in the end, as ineffectual as the rest of us.*

*I try to imagine what your life is like now, what you do every day, what you're wearing, what you eat. I want to believe that the people who have you are misguided yet kind, that they recognize what a good man you are and treat you well. It's the way I survive day to day. It hurts too much to think of you being mistreated. If I picture you locked away somewhere and suffering, a weight descends on me that makes it almost impossible to get out of bed in the morning.*

*Your captors surely know you by now. They have*

*to recognize what a good man you are. I imagine you working with their children, telling them that you have children, too, showing them the pictures you carry in your wallet. Can't the men who have you understand how much your children miss you? How can it not matter to them?*

*How can they keep you away from us all this time? We've done what they asked, over and over again. Are they oblivious to the depth of their cruelty? What kind of people are they that they don't care?*

*I used to keep a calendar beside our bed, next to the rose you picked for me before you left. Every night I marked another day, counting how many you'd been gone. I don't do that anymore. I don't want to be reminded of all the days we'll never get back.*

*When I can't sleep at night, I tell you about my day. I imagine you hearing me and smiling over the details that make up my life now. I never tell you how defeated I feel at times, or how I work to hide it from everyone for fear they will see it as a reason to stop believing you are coming home to us.*

*And I couldn't tell you about the lump I found in my breast and how hard it was going through all the tests without you here to lean on. The lump was benign—the process reaching that diagnosis, utterly terrifying. I couldn't stop worrying about what would happen to Shelly and Jason if something happened to me.*

*We need you home.*

*I'm worn down with missing you.*

*I'm going to read this tomorrow and will probably tear it up or burn it in the fireplace. I don't want you to get the idea I ever doubted what I was doing to free you or thought the work a burden. I would gladly spend the rest of my life at it, even if, in the end, we only had one day together.*

*You are my life, Evan.*

*I will love you forever.*

# CHAPTER 11

David plucked one of the larger chunks of meat out of the canned dog food and slipped an antibiotic capsule inside. They'd decided to start the pills in the morning after seeing how agitated Pearl was over her missing pup the night before. This was his third attempt. The first pill she'd managed to leave in the bottom of a bowl that she'd otherwise licked dishwasher clean. The second attempt he made an hour later. He opened a capsule and mixed it into some canned food. She sniffed the offering, gave him a piercing look and walked outside to go to the bathroom.

"Okay," he said, placing the bowl with the hidden capsule at the closet door. "Third time's the charm."

Pearl peered around the closet door and waited until David had backed across the room, before coming out. She sniffed and tasted and ate.

David leaned his shoulder into the wall and grinned. "I win," he announced. But the victory was short-lived. Pearl abruptly stopped eating, worked her tongue around her mouth for several seconds—and popped out the pill.

"Oh, you trust me enough to move in with me," David said, venting, "but not enough to know I wouldn't poison you?"

"You two have a problem?" Julia inquired from the bedroom doorway.

David caught his breath at the sight of her, not realizing until that moment that he'd been waiting for her to come and fill his morning. "Just how important is it that she take these pills?" he asked, working hard to tone down his happiness over Julia's arrival.

"Why?"

"The only way we're going to get them into her is to pin her between us and shove them down her throat. I can see getting away with that once, but not twice."

She held out her hand. "Let me try."

"Gladly." He handed her the bottle and watched her go into the kitchen, allowing himself a moment of guilty pleasure as he admired the shape and form and movement that he'd concluded made her one of the most beautiful women he'd ever known.

Julia came back and gave the wary dog a stern frown. "Okay, Miss Pearl. We're through messing around. You're going to swallow this pill and you're *not* going to give me any grief about it. Got it?"

Pearl tilted her head to one side and stared at Julia, holding her ground while Julia approached, but the dog was poised to flee.

David shook his head in wonder when Pearl made a whimpering sound and leaned into Julia. If he believed in such things, he would swear Pearl understood.

Julia put one hand over Pearl's muzzle and with the other separated her jaws and slipped the pill to the back of her tongue. Pearl swallowed, and it was done. "Good girl," Julia said, this time scratching Pearl's chin. She reached into her pocket and pulled out a piece of leftover chicken she'd taken from the refrigerator. Pearl accepted the peace offering, tucked her nose under Julia's hand for one last scratch and went into the closet to check on her pup.

"That was impressive," David said.

"Eighteen years on a farm and you learn a thing or two about how to deal with stubborn animals." She walked past David on her way into the living room. He followed. "I'm going into town to pick up a couple of things and check the mail. Is there anything you need?"

"Give me a minute and I'll go with you."

"Really?" Even as friendly as they'd become lately, she seemed surprised. "I would have asked, but knew you worked in the morning."

"I'm done. I got up early."

She glanced at the couch. "Not comfortable?"

Nothing got by her. "I figured I'd let Pearl have a day or two to get used to sharing the house before I moved back into the bedroom."

"Keep this up and I'm going to think there's a tender heart beating under that grumpy exterior," she teased.

He felt an idiotic pleasure at both her opinion and the teasing. "I just don't want her to disappear and leave me with a puppy to raise."

"Uh-huh." She headed out the door. "Meet me at the car in fifteen minutes. I have a couple of phone calls I need to make first."

Instead of following the shoreline, the easier route back to her house, Julia went through the forest. She loved the snapping sounds the dry pine needles and fallen branches made with each footfall. And she loved the smell. The pine reminded her of Christmas. Flashes of memories from Christmases with Evan landed and melted like giant snowflakes drifting onto an upturned face. He'd loved Christmas, finally understanding the joy of the season when he joined her family, becoming a rabid participant when they started their own family. He was the one who took out the decorations and put up the lights and played the music. And he was the one who dragged them out of the house to walk hand in hand on frosty evenings through garishly overdecorated neighborhoods.

Knowing Evan would want her to, she'd tried to keep up their traditions for Shelly and Jason, but it wasn't the same without him.

There were boxes in her closet filled with handmade Christmas and birthday presents for Evan that would never be opened. One day, when Shelly and Jason had homes and families of their own, Julia would give them the gifts they had made for their father.

To think that they might not remember Evan the way he deserved to be remembered broke her heart. But how could she expect them to live in the past and still embrace the future? As desperately as she missed their company in her loneliness, she loved her children too much to have them live with her in this world of constant sorrow.

Which, she reminded herself a dozen times a day, was why she was here now. Her struggle to find a way to let go of Evan and be the mother they needed was something she had to do for them and without them. It would have been easier without David as such a poignant, real reminder of what it had been like to have someone to share her day-to-day life with.

She was on the front porch when she heard the phone ring. It was Barbara. "I was just about to call you," she said.

"Great minds," Barbara replied.

"So, when are you coming for a visit?"

"How about this weekend?"

"Are you serious?" She squealed in delight. So much for calm and rational and convincing the family she was doing just fine without them. "That's great. I can't wait to see you. How long can you stay?"

"Until Monday. We have the day off for some administration thing."

With her old car on its last legs, Barbara had signed up to teach summer school to earn a down payment for a new one. "I can't wait to see you," Julia repeated. "You'll love it here. It's so beautiful and peaceful. And there's a boat. We could go fishing."

"Fishing? Me? Are you insane?"

"Well, then we'll just row around the lake. There's this family of geese you have to see and there's—"

Barbara laughed. "You don't have to sell me, Julia. I'll be there. And, if it's okay, I'm bringing someone with me."

"Of course it's okay," she said, her words more generous than her feelings. She didn't want to have to share her sister. "Who is it?"

"A guy."

Julia's jaw dropped. She'd been so wrapped up in

herself she hadn't even known Barbara was seeing someone. "When did this happen?"

"A couple of months ago. Things are moving along pretty fast and I decided it was time you two met."

"Wow. This is great." Julia hoped she sounded more enthusiastic than she felt. She wasn't sure she was ready to witness love in bloom, especially not with someone she counted on emotionally as much as Barbara.

*God, could she really be that selfish?*

"I can't wait to meet him," Julia said, this time meaning it.

"I realize this is hard for you, Julia," Barbara said. "But I also know it would have been harder if you'd found out later that I was dating a special guy and hadn't told you. I want you to be a part of this now."

"You're right. Of course. And I am happy for you." She could do this. She had to. Barbara had been with her through every moment of every crisis for five and a half years. Her sister deserved this happiness. How could she know that the timing was so bad, that Julia had met a man who filled her with a renewed and desperate hunger for what she could no longer have?

"I can't wait for you to meet him. His name is Michael St. John and he's an English professor at Sacramento State. A *teacher,* Julia. How perfect is that?"

"That's wonderful," Julia managed to say. "But be

forewarned, he's going to have to be really special in my eyes to be good enough for you."

Barbara laughed happily. "I'm not the least bit worried. You're going to love him."

They talked a few minutes more, discussed what food Barbara should bring and the best time to arrive and said goodbye. Julia returned the receiver to its cradle and sat down at the kitchen table. She had planned to call her mother but had no idea how much she knew about Barbara's new man. If she said the wrong thing or nothing at all, she could wind up with both of them angry at her. Their family dynamics were like a pinball game, one loose ball and the whole board would light up.

"Are you in there?" David called through the screen door.

Julia glanced at the clock. A half hour had passed with her splashing around in a pond of self-pity over Barbara's wonderful news. Thank God no one had seen her. She jumped up and knocked over the chair. "Coming," she shouted.

Drawn by the noise, David appeared beside her. "Are you okay?"

"Yes, of course." Tears spilled down her cheeks. Damn, damn—*damn it*. She turned her back to him and righted the chair. "What makes you think I'm not?" She lost all credibility when she couldn't stifle the sob that came next.

In a move that took them both by surprise, David reached for her. "I'm not very good at this kind of thing," he said self-consciously. "And I'll deny it if you ever remind me I said something this cheesy, but you look like you could use a hug."

Instead of pushing him away, something she would have sworn she would have done, she buried her face in his shoulder, closed her eyes and breathed in the smell of the man holding her. He was the same height as Evan and had the same build, but didn't hold her as close or as intimately as Evan would have. The way she desperately wanted to be held.

The moment should have been awkward. It should have felt wrong. But it was neither.

His arms still around her, David asked, "Have you had breakfast?"

She almost laughed at the question. It was so like the men she knew to look for a good exit line rather than just leave. Stepping from his arms, she wiped her eyes. "I usually don't—"

"Yeah, I figured. But I know this terrific place on the river that makes the best sourdough pancakes in town, and it's late enough you could call it lunch."

"The best pancakes in *this* town?" She was dizzyingly grateful that he hadn't gone where she would have let him go. She was vulnerable and confused and ached for real intimacy. She would have used David, and he was too special for that to happen.

He grinned. "Okay, so that's not much of a boast."

"I'll go if you'll do something for me."

"Sounds fair," he said.

"Come to dinner Saturday."

He waited for her to go on, seemingly sensing there was more.

"My sister and a friend, a male friend, a new male friend, are going to be here for the weekend and I want someone to..." She didn't know how to tell him what she needed without appearing pathetic.

"You need someone to shift the focus from lust-filled gazes and groping under the table to sensible things like the weather?"

"Yes," she admitted. "It's not that I'm not happy for my sister—"

"You just don't want it shoved in your face."

She let out a sigh. "That makes me seem so selfish."

"So what? I'd say you've more than earned the right."

Again, tears welled in her eyes. They weren't the pretty words she would have heard from her family or friends, empty words of understanding meant to ease her pain. She'd known David two weeks, but she'd learned he was too pragmatic to waste time spouting something he didn't believe.

"I have, haven't I?" she said. "Well?"

For the question to register took a second. "You drive a hard bargain, Mrs. McDonald. This dinner party of yours sounds about as stimulating as chaperoning a high-school prom."

"You want stimulating? What if I told you I'm fully prepared to dazzle you with a discussion on quarks." From somewhere she found a grin. "I sat next to a man on a flight to Colombia who actually studied them for a living. It was a very, very long flight."

"And that's supposed to tempt me?"

"Just how hungry are you for these pancakes?"

He laughed. "Okay, it's a deal."

Two days later David went into town with Julia to retrieve Francis from the vet. He was a much different dog from the one she had left, squirming, nuzzling, yipping and trying to suckle anything and everything he could fit in his mouth, including Julia's earlobe. The vet had purposely withheld his last feeding, leaving him ready and eager for his mom.

Pearl must have sensed their approach because she met them on the porch when they returned, dancing in circles and calling out in a high, rapid whine. There was no way she could see her puppy wrapped inside the blanket Julia carried, but it was obvious she knew he was there.

Francis squirmed until his head popped free, answering Pearl's call with frantic yips. Julia waited until they were in the bedroom to put Francis down. Pearl immediately sniffed and licked him from head to toe, turning him on his back and then on his stomach, talking the entire time, her thin body trembling with joy. Satisfied, she gently picked him up in her mouth and carried him into the closet. Seconds later she had settled and was feeding her family.

Julia heard a deep contented sigh between the suckling sounds. She looked at David. He was standing with his shoulder pressed against the door frame, looking back at her.

He smiled. "All in all, I'd say this ranks pretty damn close to winning the lottery."

She returned his smile. "Higher."

"Seems to me we should be doing something to celebrate."

"What did you have in mind?"

"Dinner? I know a little restaurant in town that makes the best—"

She laughed. "Is it as good as the pancake house?"

"Better."

"Give me a half hour to get ready."

He did a quick appraisal. "You look fine." He cleared his throat. "Better than fine. You look beautiful."

She brought her hand up to her hair, a silly, feminine gesture, an automatic response to the unexpected compliment. No one had told her she looked beautiful since… Since Evan. Just as unexpectedly, her cheeks burned with a sudden blush. She thanked him because it seemed the least awkward thing to do and then insisted on the half hour, needing it now to regain her equilibrium.

*Three Years Missing*

*I'm back, Evan. I've worked my way through the tunnel of depression I was in and am out the other side. I'm sorry it took so long. I considered not telling you, but we've always shared everything, good or bad, and I finally decided it was wrong to pretend I've been this never-failing, constant pillar of strength. It's four o'clock in the morning here, which means it's seven where you are. I'm trying to picture what your day will be like today. I want to believe you're doing something that makes you happy, so I pull out some of my favorite fantasies—that you are teaching kids math, or showing men how to bring clean water to their village—things that will give you a sense of accomplishment when you're home again and reflecting back at the time you spent in Colombia.*

*I'm sitting up in bed, a cup of coffee in one hand, a pen in the other, your rose in a vase on the nightstand, keeping me company and triggering the most wonderful memories. Not that I have to have a trigger. You are always with me, Evan. I feel your presence in the air I breathe. I hear your whispered words of love and longing when the leaves rustle in the oak tree and when the birds call for me to fill their feeder. You hold me in my dreams and give me the strength and comfort I need to wake and face another day without you.*

*A storm is blowing outside. The rain is hitting the*

*windows in crashing waves that sound like your favorite Storm Giant is back, tossing handfuls of sand against the panes. Do you remember telling Jason that story when he was four and woke up terrified by his first really big storm? You might have gotten away with it if you hadn't started with the embellishments. I never did understand why it was necessary to give the Storm Giant great big teeth. How could that be a guy thing?*

*He still remembers your giant, Evan. I overhead him telling his friend Shawn about it the other day. Shelly doesn't remember that night, but then you didn't scare the crap out of her the way you did Jason.*

*All those years we worked so hard to create big-deal, carefully planned, expensive memories, and this is the kind of thing that sticks. Go figure.*

*With Shelly it's all the weekends she spent working with you in your gardens. She's always spotting some new flower or bush that she's going to tell you about when you're home. We're going to need a couple of acres to accommodate everything she's written in the notebook she's saving for you.*

*I get so angry sometimes when I think of all you've missed and how much richer our children's lives would be if you were here with them. It's been three years now, Evan. Three years. When I break it into days and weeks and months, they overwhelm me.*

*I have wrinkles I didn't have when you left. And even though I've lost a few pounds, my stomach isn't as flat as it used to be. Stupid things like this hit me at the strangest moments. I know they don't matter, but they're like height markings on a closet door, indicating the years we've been apart. I still find myself reaching for the phone to call you at work and share something inconsequential that happened during the day.*

*It's not the big things you're missing that bother me as much as the small moments that make up our children's lives. We're the only ones who truly care about most of what I'd say. Telling you about Shelly shaving her legs for the first time isn't the same as being here for that tiny milestone on her path to becoming a full-grown woman.*

*And I never expected to have to shop for jock straps for Jason. I was so upset that I had to do something that you should have been doing I actually broke down in the middle of the sporting-goods store. Try explaining that to a bunch of people jostling one another to get to the two-for-one athletic-shoe sale.*

*Is there a religion I don't know about where prayers have a more direct line to God?*

# CHAPTER 12

Barbara brought her wine into the kitchen and stood within whispering distance of Julia. "Okay, you want to tell me more about this David guy?"

"There's nothing to tell. He's the caretaker, I owed him a favor, so I invited him to dinner."

"Now ask me how much of that I believe."

Julia handed Barbara a bowl of mashed potatoes. "Here, make yourself useful."

Barbara put the bowl on the counter. "Not until you spill who this guy really is and what he means to you. *And,* why do you owe him a favor?"

"He's the caretaker. He means nothing to me." That brought a jolt, forcing her to acknowledge, if only to herself, that David meant more to her than she'd ever imagined another man could mean. "And he picked up tonight's roast when he went into town yesterday to get the mail. I could hardly ask him to pick up the meat for a dinner party and not invite him."

"You could if he was 'just' the caretaker."

"Give it a rest, Barbara. As much as you'd like to believe otherwise, love is not contagious." This time she handed her sister the green salad. "Now, go—before it wilts."

Julia followed Barbara into the dining room and announced dinner. Twenty minutes later Michael sat back in his chair and proclaimed himself stuffed.

"Wonderful dinner, Julia," Michael said. "Barbara said you were a great cook, but this was extraordinary."

"Thank you." She'd decided she liked Michael. He was a couple of years older than Barbara, divorced but not bitter, had an offbeat sense of humor that perfectly matched Barbara's own sense of fun and was obviously head over heels in love with her sister.

Michael held up his wineglass and tilted it toward David. "And the wine is exceptional. I don't think I've ever had better, and I was married to a woman who wrote for *The Wine Spectator*."

David acknowledged the compliment with a nod. "All I know about wine is what I like."

"Evan loved port," Julia said. "The first time I had it I thought it tasted like cough syrup, but it grew on me."

"I'm not there yet," David said. "I've had what people swore was the best and it still didn't do anything for me. What did Evan see in it?"

Julia laughed. "He only knew what he liked, too. He couldn't tell you why."

Barbara looked from Julia to David and back again, questions and curiosity burning in her eyes. "Evan was a special man," she said, plainly testing.

"So I've heard," David told her.

Julia knew exactly what Barbara was thinking, and would make another attempt to set her straight as soon as they were alone again. The last thing she wanted was for Barbara to leave believing there was something going on between her and David. Barbara would be on her cell phone calling their mother the second she was within range of a tower.

Michael leaned forward and rested his elbows on the table. "How long have you been working here, David?"

"Almost a year."

"And before that?"

"Here and there."

"Sorry, I didn't mean to pry. It's just that you seem so familiar to me and I was trying to figure out where we might have met."

"I've lived on the East Coast for the past few years."

In an obvious eureka moment, Michael slapped his hands together in triumph and grinned. "I've got it. You're Nicolas Golden."

David glanced at Julia and waited for what seemed an eternity before reluctantly admitting, "Guilty."

Julia frowned. She recognized the name but not why. "I'm confused. You're not David Prescott?"

"That's my real name," David said. "Nicolas Golden is a pseudonym."

"I still don't—"

"Oh, my God, Julia," Barbara said. "How could you not know the name Nicolas Golden?"

"You must have read him in college," Michael added. "Everyone did. He's considered one of the most influential writers of the past twenty years."

David put his wineglass back on the table. "There are plenty of people who would argue that point," he said, shifting position, clearly uncomfortable. "Me among them."

Julia's heart went out to him. Had she realized, she would have warned him that of all her friends and family, she'd asked him to share a meal with the two people most likely to figure out who he was.

"*Flying on Clipped Wings* is my all-time favorite book," Barbara said. "I've almost worn out my original copy."

"You wrote *Flying on Clipped Wings?* You're *that* Nicolas Golden?" Julia gasped. She'd first read the book when she was a freshman, and remembered being so impressed with the ideas and anger and compassion contained in the slim volume that she'd fallen a little in love with the man she imagined the writer to be. She'd told Evan. He'd laughed and told her that it was okay—he was a little in love with the guy, too.

"Why didn't you tell me?" Julia immediately regretted the question. He didn't owe her that kind of revelation or explanation.

David shrugged helplessly, trapped into answering by social convention. "It's my past. It has nothing to do with who I am now."

"I'm disappointed to hear that," said Michael. "I was hoping the long absence meant a new book would be out soon."

"You retired?" Barbara said. "To become a caretaker?" The insensitivity of the question must have occurred to her as soon as she asked it, because before David had a chance to answer, Barbara added, "Pardon me a second while I get my foot out of my mouth. I really didn't mean that the way it sounded. I was just hoping you were here for the peace and quiet so you could work on a new book."

"Or that you were doing research," Michael said.

"You weren't sent here by my agent by any chance, were you?" David asked.

Feeling protective, Julia decided he'd been put through enough and interrupted. "I'm sorry to break things up, but David and I are already an hour late giving Pearl her evening pill." She stood. "Why don't you go into the living room and finish the wine," she said to Barbara and Michael. "I'll make coffee and we can have dessert when David and I get back."

She retrieved her sweater from the closet and looked back to see Barbara and Michael clearing the table. "Please, leave it," she said, even knowing she would be ignored.

"I'm sorry," Barbara mouthed.

Julia gave her a tiny shrug. David held the door and followed her through. They were halfway across the lawn when he said, "You didn't have to do that. I can take care of myself."

Before Julia had a chance to reply, Barbara came out on the porch and called her. "Julia—Shelly's on the phone. Do you want me to tell her you'll get back to her later?"

Julia hesitated. It surprised her. Evan was the only person she'd ever put in front of Shelly or Jason.

"Take the call," David told her before she had a chance to answer. "It could be something important. I'll wait for you at the house."

She and Shelly had talked that afternoon and it was unlike her to call again this soon just to chat. Julia nodded to David and told Barbara, "I'm coming." She ran back across the lawn, avoiding her sister's questioning look as she passed her on the way into the house.

"Hi," she said into the receiver. "What's up?"

"Not much."

"You just called to say hi?" She peered out the kitchen window and watched as David disappeared into the trees.

"Not exactly. I met a guy at Grandpa's Grange meeting last week and he asked me to go to the movie with him tomorrow night. Grandma said I had to talk to you first. I told her you wouldn't care if she didn't care, but—" she dropped her voice to a whisper "—you know how Grandma is."

"Does this guy have a name?"

"Steve."

"A last name?" She struggled to keep the impatience out of her voice.

"Boehm."

"Ellis Boehm's son?" Ellis was the only boy at her high school who'd actually spent a whole night in jail. He'd done a complete about face afterward, married her best friend, Karol, the day after graduation, became a policeman after finishing community college, worked his way up to chief in six years and made a successful run for mayor—all before he'd turned thirty. She'd met his kids and liked them a lot.

"I don't know whose son he is," Shelly whined. "I don't want a long-term relationship with the guy. I just want to see a movie with him."

"Ask Grandma if he's Ellis's son. If he is, you can go. If he's not, call me back."

"This is so dumb. What possible difference does it make who his father is?"

"Shelly?"

"Yeah?"

"How badly do you want to go?"

"Enough to shut up and do what I'm told?"

Julia smiled. "Wow, for me to get that out of you this guy must really be cute."

"*Cute,* Mom? Please. You know that word makes me gag."

"Well? Is he?"

"I guess so," she reluctantly admitted. "He looks a lot like Dad when he was in high school. At least, the way he looked in that picture Grandma has on the piano when Dad's hair was long and he wore that black leather jacket you keep in the closet at home."

Julia swallowed, hard. She wasn't sure whether the comparison was good or bad, only that it was a connection Shelly had made to her father. She worried, too much at times, that Shelly and Jason would forget Evan now that he was no longer the constant presence in their lives that he had been all the years he was only missing and not dead. "Call me when you get home tomorrow night."

"It could be late."

"It better not be that late. I have two hours on you. There's no way I'll be in bed by the time you should be home."

"Love you, Mom."

Shelly was through talking. "I love you, too, Shelly."

She made a dash for the door before Barbara could corner her and ask the questions Julia saw bubbling in her eyes. "Be right back. Pearl will eat David alive if I'm not there to intercede." A little melodramatic, and a little unfair to Pearl, but it accomplished what Julia needed.

David used a fork to dig out the third of a can of wet dog food he used to mix with the half cup of kibble, added a little water to create a paste and sprinkled a teaspoon of the powdered vitamins over the top. Pearl must have heard the preparations because she came to the kitchen door to watch him.

"How're the kids?" David asked.

She tilted her head and stared at him.

"Glad to hear it." He'd been trying to convince himself that she was coming around a little and would one day let him touch her.

"Since you ask, things were going great for me tonight, too. Right up to the part where Julia—" Pearl tilted her head to the other side. "Yes, I'm talking about your Julia. Like I said, things were going great—right up to the minute where it all went to hell. Now Julia has every reason not to trust me, any more than—well, any more than you do."

Julia tapped on the door frame before coming inside.

He glanced up, acknowledging her presence. "I don't know why they can't make antibiotics that taste like these vitamins. She does fine with this stuff."

"I trust you," she said, ignoring his offer of a neutral opening. "You didn't owe me anything you didn't want to tell me."

David took a towel off the counter and wiped his hands. "I let you think I was someone I'm not."

"So does this mean the real you wouldn't sleep on a couch six inches too short in order to make a homeless dog feel safe? Or maybe the real you would never listen to the ramblings of a woman frozen in sorrow and indecision. Or could it be that the real you doesn't—"

He held up his hand. "Enough."

"Why did you come to my place tonight? I told you Michael was an English professor. You must have realized he—"

Knowing it would be a mistake to give her the real answer—that he'd begun looking for any reasonable excuse to be with her—he said, "It's been so long since I had a book out that I thought I was safe. People have short memories." He shrugged. "Hope springs eternal?" He picked up Pearl's bowl and stared at Julia. "There are a hundred clichés that fit. You interested in hearing more?"

"Do you really not understand how important

you were to our generation? How those who weren't caught up in the 'me' thing in the eighties looked to you to say what no one else was saying back then?"

"How could I not know that, Julia?" he said in a flash of frustration. "I heard it so often I almost started believing it myself." He reached for the pills and handed them to her.

"Just because it's hard for you to hear doesn't mean it's not true."

"Let it go," he warned. "There isn't anything you can say that I haven't heard. I don't want to hear it again. Especially not from you."

She recoiled. "*Especially* me? What's that supposed to mean?"

He shook his head and moved to step around her. "Nothing."

"Oh, no, you don't." She followed him. "I thought we were friends. Friends don't say things like that and walk away."

He put the bowl on the coffee table and turned on her. "Can you really be this dense? Has losing Evan made you so myopic that you can't see what other people around you are feeling?"

"You're going to have to be a little less obtuse, David. I really don't know what you're talking about."

He was on the verge of making a huge mistake. She wasn't ready to hear how he felt about her. "If you're really my friend, you'll let it go."

Conflicted, she backed off. "All right. If that's what you want."

"It is." He motioned toward Pearl. "You first."

Julia took a pill and slipped it into Pearl's mouth, then spent a minute talking to her. David handed her the bowl of food and she and the dog disappeared into his bedroom.

When she returned, she hesitated, obviously wanting to say something more but unsure how to say it. "There's coffee and lemon pie...but I don't suppose you're interested."

"Not tonight," he said.

"Tomorrow?"

"Probably not."

"I understand." She started to leave.

"Julia?"

"Yes?"

"Would you—" He was torn between protecting himself and making her a part of the problem. Her sister and Michael could go home and tell a thousand people that they'd seen him and it likely wouldn't matter. But if just one of those people had a connection to someone who had a connection to someone who did care, his freedom and isolation would be over. "Never mind."

"Are you sure?"

He nodded. "It's nothing."

"They won't tell anyone they saw you, David," she

said, guessing what he was going to ask. "I'm going to talk to them about it before they leave."

"I'm sorry I put you in that position."

"You didn't put me anywhere I didn't want to be." She placed her hands on his shoulders, stood on tiptoe and kissed his cheek. "It's what friends do for each other."

He shoved his hands in his pockets to keep from reaching for her. "Then thank you for being my friend."

"You're welcome." She moved to leave, but instead stopped and gazed at David for a long time. "Evan loved *Flying on Clipped Wings*. You two would have been great friends. You have a lot in common."

More than she would ever realize. "Julia?"

"Yes?"

He held out his hand. She hesitated for several seconds before slipping her hand into his. He drew her to him, waiting for her to resist, ready to admit it was too soon. But she didn't. She came willingly, tilting her chin up when he brought her against his chest, parting her lips in sweet anticipation when he kissed her.

It was everything he could do to hold back, knowing the depth of his need, the breadth of his growing love, would scare her. She put her arms around his neck and held him, deepening the kiss almost to the point of commitment, giving him reason to hope.

And then it was over.

Julia's arms slid from his neck. She touched his cheek and looked into his eyes. "I wish…" She choked back a sob. "Oh, David, there's no way for me to tell you how much I wish this could be."

He took her hands in his. "Yeah, me, too."

"I'm sorry." There were tears in her eyes.

He believed her.

*Four Years Missing*

*I considered waiting until you were home to tell you this—which is a good indication of how strongly I believe you can hear my thoughts as I write them—but I figured you might as well know now. I bought an artificial Christmas tree.*

*Are you groaning? Screaming in protest?*

*It's beautiful, Evan. They're making them so much more realistic now. And, best of all, they come with the lights already attached. It took me and the kids half the time to put up the tree this year. I told everyone there were lots of reasons I made the change, but the truth is that it just wasn't the same picking out a tree without you. And I did such a bad job of securing last year's tree in the stand that it fell over in the middle of the night. I thought someone had broken in the house and I called 9-1-1.*

*The cops were really nice about the false alarm, but Jason is still annoyed that I refused to let him check out the house before I contacted them. He's going through another superhero stage and thinks he's invincible. I swear I've never told him that he's the "man of the family" with you away. You know I don't believe in things like that. Well, it appears it doesn't matter. Jason feels protecting me and Shelly is something you would want him to do. How can I argue with that?*

*Shelly's changing so fast lately that I tell one girl*

*good-night and wake up to find another one in her place. In less than a year she's gone from being a pretty little girl to knocking on the door of being a full-fledged beautiful woman. That fourteen-year-old-hormone-influenced mind that's trapped inside a Victoria's Secret body terrifies me at times. Ninety percent of her conversations with her girlfriends is about boys and the other ten percent is about cell phones and iPods.*

*Were there iPods before you were kidnapped? I can't remember for sure. As much as you love listening to music when you're working in the garden, you're going to love all the new technology. You can go online and buy almost any song for less than a dollar. What fun it will be for the three of us to bring you up-to-date and teach you how to operate all the new gadgets.*

*Have I told you lately how much I love to watch you with our kids? There's a secret that women have had forever that either men don't know or choose to ignore. We think men who are good with children are incredibly sexy. It's such a turn-on to see a father nurturing his son or daughter. Give us a guy who isn't afraid to hold a baby or roll around on the grass with a giggling three-year-old or walk to school holding hands with his kindergartner and we're butter in a hot pan, melting and sizzling at the same time. So there you have it, my magnificent stud muffin, the secret to your power over me. Just thinking about you with Shelly and Jason turns me to mush.*

*Of course it doesn't hurt that you're tall, dark and handsome, but when I look back at memories we share with the kids, I feel such fierce longing for you that I can hardly breathe.*

*How is it that your shoulders never gave out at parades with one of them and then the other perched there for hours? And how did your arms hold up carrying them back from one of our walks in the mountains when they grew too tired or sleepy to make it on their own? How much sleep did you get when you crawled into bed with one of them after they'd had a bad dream? Did you ever regret not being a better golfer because you gave up your weekends with the guys to coach Shelly's and then Jason's soccer teams?*

*Do you see your little brother, Shawn, in them? Are you memorializing him by doing for your own children what you couldn't do for him? We should have named Jason after Shawn, but I was too young to think of something that seems so obvious now. And I'm sorry I didn't ask you about him more. I was always afraid it would bring up sad memories.*

*Since you've been gone, I've learned I was wrong to worry about that. Memories are our connections. When they are of people we love, they are the wheat that makes the bread that sustains us.*

*I was thinking the other day that when you're*

*home again, we should plant a garden for Shawn, one filled with all his favorite colors. Do you remember what they were? Was he old enough to have favorite colors before he died? I guess what I'm really asking is, did he have colorful things to play with? When I think of the place you lived with him and your mother, all I see is gray and black and white.*

*I even have the location picked out for Shawn's garden. It's where we buried your mouse, underneath the peppermint-candy crepe myrtle. I didn't tell you about the mouse before because I didn't want to write anything sad. Are you laughing at that? He hung around for almost three years. According to something I read, that's an incredibly long time for a wild mouse. He must have been a young teenager when he wound up in Shelly's room. I found him one morning under the feeder, tucked into a sleeping position on top of a leaf. I cried. But then, I cry pretty easily these days.*

*Jason insisted on a funeral—your mouse had become a pretty regular part of our lives, fearlessly feasting on the birdseed that dropped from the feeder. He would even come out when we were there, paying us no more mind than he would a pill bug. Shelly attended the ceremony, reluctantly, grumbling the whole time and never getting closer than ten feet. Later, when she thought she was alone, I saw her putting flowers on the grave. She was wiping her eyes when she left.*

# CHAPTER 13

*Six Weeks Later*

Julia sat on the railing that surrounded her porch and watched for David. He'd taken Francis and Josi on a long walk to wear them out, hoping they would sleep on the flight to Sacramento. There they had a three-hour layover and a planned playtime to wear them out again for the direct, five-hour flight to New York, all carefully worked out to put him on the only airline that would let him have both dogs in the passenger compartment.

Somehow, from somewhere, David had found the answers he'd come there seeking, and had packed away the computer weeks ago, content, at last, with not writing. He claimed he'd let go without guilt or regret, but not without a certain sadness. When Julia expressed disappointment, he'd pointed out that he'd packed his laptop, not tossed it.

He was going home to sell his apartment and rid himself of the trappings he'd let accumulate over the years. Then would come a motor home just big enough for him and the "kids." Stealing a page from John Steinbeck's book *Travels With Charley,* he was going to reintroduce himself to a country and its people he'd only known by its coasts for the past twenty years.

He'd promised to keep in touch, because Julia had said she wanted him to. He even told her he would visit if he ever found himself in her neighborhood. After all, she'd put so much time into helping raise Pearl's pups it was only fair that she got to see the magnificent dogs they were sure to become.

It would take DNA to convince an outsider that Pearl was related in any way to the two wildly gregarious puppies that had consumed David's house and life. She'd obviously crossed paths with one of the breeds of short-haired pointers, because they looked like pet-quality examples of their father and nothing like her.

Over the past four weeks, as Pearl had weaned her pups she had moved in with Julia, first by minutes, then by hours and finally completely, leaving Francis and Josi to David. She let Julia give her a bath and luxuriated in the one-on-one time that came with her daily brushing. All the attention, regular meals and freedom from stress left her looking like a dog that had never known anything but a loving home.

Julia had never felt such a strong, empathetic connection to an animal before Pearl. It was as if their life experiences had created an understanding that went deeper than the words that usually formed a friendship this deep. When Pearl lay beside Julia's chair on the porch, her head on her paws, staring into the forest, Julia felt her sorrow and longing as readily as she felt her own and knew without question that there had been more puppies Pearl hadn't been able to save. When Julia was caught up in thinking about what should have been, invariably Pearl wound up at her side.

Drawn by Julia's thoughts, Pearl got up, crossed the porch and nosed Julia's hand. She looked down into expressive, questioning eyes. "I'm going to miss David," she admitted. "I know it's time for him to go and I know it's right, but that doesn't make it any easier."

She held Pearl's muzzle and locked gazes. "And I'm going to miss Francis and Josi, too. Oh, Pearl, what are we going to do with ourselves without the three of them around here?"

Pearl responded with a throaty whine.

A familiar sound drew their attention as the pups came crashing through the trees, attacking each other, fighting and knocking each other over, tumbling and getting up to do it all over again. Seconds later David followed them, shaking his head.

Julia laughed. "I see you managed to wear them out. They certainly appear exhausted."

"And here I thought it was just my imagination."

"What did you feed them this morning?"

"Steroids and uppers, from the looks of it." The instant they spotted Pearl, the pups made a dash for her, taking the porch steps two at a time, missing almost as often as not with nosedives into the runners, gaining their balance and lunging forward again. Pearl issued a guttural warning, which they completely ignored, one jumping up to grab her good ear, the other tackling her tail.

"It's their way of telling her they love her," David supplied, climbing the steps after them.

Pearl let out another growl.

"Which I'm sure just means that she loves them, too," Julia said.

He sat beside her. "I wonder if she'll miss them."

"Yes," Julia said with absolute conviction. Just as she would miss David, more than she wanted to admit—to him or to herself. But by mutual agreement and understanding, certain things were left unspoken between them.

"It's been a good summer," he said simply.

"For me, too," she said.

"I got up this morning and tried to decide what was important enough to say to you before I leave. I've been going over them all day, but, basically, there's just one that matters." He took her hand. "I came here looking for the man I used to be. You helped me see that letting him go is my road to freedom. Thanks to you, for the first time in longer than I can remember I'm looking forward instead of back."

"I hesitate telling you this, but my mother insists we didn't meet by accident this summer. She's convinced some cosmic force brought us together—" She gave him a self-conscious smile. "Are you ready for this?"

He returned her smile. "Lay it on me."

"To heal each other's souls."

"And you don't believe her?"

She was surprised to see that he wasn't teasing her; he really wanted to know. "It's hard for me to listen when she starts in. All my life she's insisted nothing happens by chance and that all I have to do is pay attention and I'll see the hidden meanings in everything from the ordinary to the bizarre. It sounds mean, but I finally reached the point where I just tune her out."

"I don't know about cosmic forces," he said. "But if you think about the series of circumstances it took to bring us together at this time and this place, you have to wonder if there wasn't something going on."

David had never believed in premonitions or signs or omens, either, but he believed in coincidence even less. If there was some mystical force that brought them together, it could have worked a little harder on some of the more important details. Or was loving Julia and knowing she would never love him in return the coin he had to pay for his newfound peace of mind?

"I have a feeling there's another time and place where you'll find the right woman waiting for you, David."

A flash of anger shot through him at the pat sentiment. How could she dismiss his feelings so casually? But then he saw that they weren't just words; she actually believed what she'd said.

She smiled. "Wrong thing to say?"

"Am I so transparent?"

"At times."

"I'll get over you, Julia." He meant it to reassure her, a promise between friends.

"I know." She squeezed his hand.

He glanced at his watch. He'd hired one of the vet assistants to drive him to the airport in Redding because he owned a van big enough to hold two dog carriers and luggage. He was due to arrive in ten minutes. "I'd better get going. I want to get the 'kids' loaded and settled before we take off."

"One more minute," she said. "I have something for you."

She went inside, brought out a package and handed it to him. Seeing how it was wrapped, in discarded manuscript pages that she'd unfolded and taped together, he shot her a questioning look.

"I stole them from your trash," she admitted.

He removed the bow, a pine cone decorated with tufts of Pearl's hair and held in place with fishing line, and then the paper. Inside was an unframed photograph of Julia and Pearl sitting on the top step of the porch, Julia's arm around Pearl, Pearl leaning into her side. Underneath the photograph were three bright red, spiral-bound journals. David caught his breath at the stab of emotion in his chest.

"For when the words come back." Julia smiled. "I looked at a lot of fancy leather-bound journals when I went into Redding last week, but these seemed more your style."

"They're perfect." He heard the crunching sound of tires on gravel and felt a profound sadness, aware their time together was over. "Thank you, Julia. For everything."

She kissed him. The touch of her lips held none of the promise that could have kept him there. When she broke the kiss and stepped away, he softly told her, "I'm going to miss you."

"Thank you for being my friend, David. I know how hard that's been for you."

"Maybe those Fates of your mother's will arrange for us to meet again one day."

She shook her head. "I think once is all we're allowed."

"I left something for you on the table at the cabin."

She raised her eyebrows in question.

"That wooden box I made. I took out the bad reviews and burned them. The box isn't anything special, but I've carried it around a lot of years and thought you might like it." David heard a car door slam. "It's time, Julia."

"Not yet. I'll help you get—"

"Now. I don't want to remember you standing on the road, watching me leave."

She nodded, tears filling her eyes. "Goodbye, David."

He turned and left, the puppies following without being called. Pearl went to Julia and sat down, one haunch planted on her foot.

"How are we going to get up tomorrow morning, knowing they won't be here?"

*Four Years, Three Hundred Sixty-four Days Missing*

*Tomorrow is an anniversary, Evan. It's not one I ever wanted to celebrate. It will be five years since you left for Colombia. I dread it. I don't believe it. I feel like screaming in frustration over all the days that turned into weeks that turned into months and now years. Why aren't you home when, with the exception of a woman abducted two months ago, every other American kidnapped before and after you has been released? What did I do wrong? Why are you still there and not home with me and Shelly and Jason?*

*It can't be your fault you're still not home; it has to be mine. I'm so sorry, Evan.*

*I don't know what else to do, so I'm starting over. I'm going back to Colombia after the holidays and I'm going to hire a new negotiator—not because I doubt the people who have worked so long and hard for us up to now. They've been incredible, giving everything they had to give and more. But I'm hoping someone new will bring new ideas and new contacts.*

*I have to do something.*

*I won't ever quit, Evan.*

*I promise.*

# CHAPTER 14

Julia picked up the smooth branch she'd found on her walk and tossed it into the water. Pearl bounded in after it, her remarkable retrieving skills making Julia wonder if she, too, had a little short-hair pointer in her obviously mixed genetic makeup.

She'd had a sense of unease the past two days, blaming the unseasonable thunderstorm that had moved in and stalled over the mountains, each lightning strike in the dry timber a potential fire disaster. Calls to her mother and Shelly and Jason and then Barbara and her brother, Fred, did nothing to settle the strange feeling that something was going on that needed her attention. Before adding

Harold and Mary to her list and worrying them over the unexpected call, she decided she was simply missing David and the pups even more than she'd anticipated.

She'd been determined to stay at least another week after they'd left just to prove she could. It took three days before she accepted that her ability to endure the isolation didn't prove anything and she began packing. She and Pearl would leave in the morning, right after the new caretaker arrived.

Pearl left the lake and stopped to shake before racing to Julia with the stick. She barked and danced in circles, letting Julia know she was ready to go again. With two teens, two kittens and the new, livelier Pearl, theirs would be an interesting household.

Exactly what she needed.

Julia tossed the stick back into the water. But Pearl wasn't interested anymore. She stared toward the house, the fur on her back standing on end. It took more than a minute for Julia to determine what had drawn Pearl's attention—a car headed toward them.

They had company.

Figuring the new caretaker had decided to arrive a day early, Julia started back to the house to meet him. She was surprised to see Harold's green Lexus pull into the driveway, instead. He got out of the car and came toward her.

Her instant smile disappeared when she noticed the look on his face. Her heart in her throat, she demanded, "What's wrong?"

"Come in the house. I have to talk to you."

*No greeting, no how are you?*

When Julia didn't move, Harold took her arm and guided her toward the house. Pearl circled them, then ran ahead, issuing a threatening growl. "It's okay, Pearl," Julia said, her voice denying her words.

Harold ignored the threatening dog and hurried Julia inside. Pearl followed, pacing between the living room and the kitchen, warily eyeing Harold.

"Sit down," Harold said.

The words snapped her out of her fog. "Enough of the melodramatics, Harold. Just tell me what's going on."

He took in a deep breath, swiped the hair off his forehead, stammered something she couldn't understand and looked at her as if she were someone to be feared. "Please, sit down."

She did, but only because he'd said it as though it really mattered.

"Evan—" He sat next to her and reached for her hands. "I don't know how to tell you this."

Now she was scared. What could he possibly tell her that was worse than what she already knew? *"Just say it."*

"He's coming home."

That didn't make sense. She stood up again. "He's already home."

"I don't know who we buried, but it wasn't Evan." He stopped to take a deep breath. "He isn't dead, Julia. I just talked to him a couple of hours ago. He was at the Embassy. They were making arrangements for a flight home." He glanced at his watch. "He's probably in the air right now."

The room was spinning. If she didn't hold on to something, she was going to fall. She put her hand out and grabbed a corner of the bookshelf. Damn it, she'd never passed out in her life and she wasn't going to now.

"Are you sure it was him?" How could it be?

Tears spilled from Harold's eyes. "Yes."

"How—"

Harold laughed through the tears and shook his head. "I don't know. All I could get out of him was that he walked out of the jungle last night and that he would tell us all about it when he got home."

"Are you absolutely sure?" She could not survive losing him twice.

"It's him, Julia," Harold insisted. "He's alive. And he's coming home."

*Evan was coming home.*

The hope she'd let die fought for footing in her mind. The pain of so many disappointments refused to yield their hold. "I want to talk to him. Why didn't you give him my number?"

"I did. He couldn't reach you."

"I don't understand—" But then she did. She looked at the phone, at the red light blinking on the answering machine. "I wasn't here," she said in a choked whisper. "How did he sound?"

"Happy—ecstatic. He couldn't stop talking about you and the kids. He was like a man diving into a swimming pool after spending a lifetime in the desert."

"Does he know that we thought he was dead?"

"The people at the Embassy told him."

"Does he know we only gave up when—" She couldn't finish.

"Aww, Julia don't do that to yourself." He gave her a helpless look. "Mary was right… I was going to have someone from town come out here to find you, but she insisted someone you cared for had to be with you when you found out."

She would have to remember to thank Mary. Again. For so many things.

"She said you'd have a hundred questions and that there was no way you should drive home alone," Harold went on, filling the silence. "We tried to reach Barbara, and when we couldn't, I finally managed to convince Mary she could trust me behind the wheel. I got here as fast as I could."

Julia went to the answering machine and, with a trembling finger, pressed Play. When she heard

Evan's voice, she let out a poignant cry of recognition and longing.

"Julia? Are you there?" He paused. "I know I'm a little late, but I thought I'd better call to make sure you got that little black dress. I'll be home soon and we've got some major celebrating to do." Another pause, this one longer. She could hear him struggle to keep from breaking down. His longing and heartache wrenched her soul. "I love you," he said softly. "I'm so sorry you had to wait all these years to hear me tell you that again."

The room took off. Her skin tingled. Stars appeared. She reached for something to hang on to again, but this time couldn't find anything. Her legs buckled. And, for the first time in her life, Julia passed out.

Julia came to with Pearl standing over her, growling fiercely, her teeth bared at Harold. "It's okay, Pearl." She struggled to a sitting position and grabbed Pearl's collar.

"You're going to have to do something about that dog," Harold said.

"How long was I out?"

"A minute, maybe two. It's a good thing you didn't hit your head or break something, because she wouldn't let me anywhere near you." He put down the blanket he'd taken off the back of the couch to try to subdue Pearl. "Is there someone you could leave her with?"

Julia ignored him and hit the button on the answering machine. She listened to Evan's voice over and over until her mind let her accept that it really was him and that he really was coming home. "I want to talk to him. Did he give you a number? Maybe I should just call the Embassy. Surely someone there would know where he is."

Harold took a piece of paper out of his pocket and read her the number. Three phone calls later she learned that Evan was indeed already on a plane and would arrive in San Francisco in five hours—too soon for her to get there to meet him. When she told Harold, he immediately arranged for a private charter to fly Evan the final hundred miles to Sacramento.

Calling her mother, working out the details to bring Shelly and Jason home, closing the house and stopping by the vet to pick up a muzzle and tranquilizer for Pearl kept Julia focused. On the long ride down the I5, she used Harold to ground her, throwing one question after another at him, even though he had few answers.

The authorities in Colombia and the United States would make the arrangements to have the man she'd buried returned to Colombia. The doctor who'd made the "positive" identification had admitted he'd lost Evan's dental and medical records and that the death certificate was based on the personal belongings found in the grave.

As soon as they were within range of a cell tower, Julia asked Harold for his phone. She hadn't bothered charging or carrying hers the months she'd been in the mountains because there wasn't any service within fifty miles of the house.

She tapped in Barbara's home number, and when her sister didn't answer tried her cell. Barbara picked up on the third ring. Her heart in her throat at what she was about to do to her sister, Julia asked, "Where are you?"

"Why?"

"Just tell me."

"I'm at the grocery store."

"Leave—right now. Get in your car, but don't start it."

"Are you okay?" Barbara asked.

*"Please,"* Julia begged. "Just do this for me. It's important. I promise you'll understand in a minute."

"You're scaring me."

"No—don't be scared."

"All right," Barbara said, switching emotional gears again. "But it better not take long. I have ice cream in my cart. The expensive kind."

In the minutes it took Barbara to assure a clerk she wasn't abandoning her cart and get to her car, Julia decided it would be better to ask her favor and then tell Barbara about Evan.

"Okay, I'm here."

"Are you inside and sitting down?"

"Wait a minute," Barbara said with a sigh. "This had better be good, Julia.

"Okay, lay it on me."

"I want you to go to Nordstrom and buy me an absolute knock-your-socks-off black dress and the sexiest black negligee you can find."

*"What?"* she nearly shouted. "This is why you dragged me out of the store? Tell me again. I can't have heard you right."

"You heard me correctly."

"Okay, I'll bite—why am I doing this?"

Julia took a deep breath. "Remember that note Evan wrote me when he left?"

"Yes… "

"He's not dead, Barbara," she somehow managed to say through the instant flood of tears. "He walked out of the jungle last night, and he's going to be home in a couple of hours."

"Julia—where are you?" The implied question was whether she'd had a breakdown and had called from a padded hospital room.

"In Harold's car. We're on our way home but won't be there in time for me to get the dress and get to the airport."

"I don't understand. How can Evan be alive when we buried him eight months ago?" Before Julia could answer, Barbara added, "Are you sure? Are you absolutely, positively sure it's Evan?"

"Yes," Julia told her. "I heard his voice. It's him, Barbara. He's coming home."

"Ohmygod—" she breathed. "Ohmygod."

Julia could hear her pounding on the steering wheel.

"This is soooo wonderful. It's beyond wonderful. It's…it's…"

"Some kind of miracle," Julia said.

"It's a hundred miracles rolled into one. Oh, Julia, I'm so far beyond words happy for you." She let out a whoop and scream so loud they should have shattered the safety glass. "Do Mom and Dad know? Of course they do—you had to call Shelly and Jason. How are the kids taking the news?"

"Shelly couldn't stop crying and Jason couldn't stop asking questions."

"And Mom and Dad?"

"Mom couldn't stop crying and Dad couldn't stop asking questions."

Barbara laughed. "Ohmygod, ohmygod, ohmygod," she squealed. "I have never been this happy. Not even close. Not in my whole life." She squealed again. "I'm going to throw a party. For all of you. Not right away," she added quickly. "In a few weeks. When Evan is ready."

"The dress?" Julia prompted.

"I'm on it— Give me a second. I'm digging for my keys."

Now it was Julia's turn to laugh. It felt like another brick had been removed from the wall she'd built around her heart. "The ice cream?"

"Oh, yeah. Okay, got it. I'll let the clerk know and then I'm outta here."

Julia heard the car door open and close. Seconds later came a long, loud horn and screeching tires. *"Barbara—"*

"Relax, that wasn't meant for me."

Just the fleeting possibility that something awful could happen to another person she loved made her sick with panic. "Promise me you'll drive carefully."

"Of course. Don't I always? Never mind—don't answer that."

"I'm going to let you go now." Barbara needed the distraction of a cell phone like she needed another dozen kids in her kindergarten class. "If you have to reach me, use Harold's cell. My battery's shot."

"Do I have a spending limit for this dress?"

"The sky," Julia said. She'd worry about how to pay for it later. "All I care about is that it's the next best thing to being naked." That so-o-o-o needed a modifier. "Within reason. You understand that, don't you?"

"This is going to be so much fun. I wish you were going with me."

"Wait for me at the house and you can help me get ready. At the moment I don't think I could manage a garter belt, let alone buttons or zippers."

"I'll keep easy entrance and exit in mind," Barbara said, dropping her voice. "For both you *and* Evan."

For the first time in almost six years Julia felt a flush crawl up her neck and knew her pale cheeks had turned a flaming crimson.

# CHAPTER 15

Harold dropped Julia and Pearl off at her house at five-thirty and returned at seven to take her to the airport. He stepped back in surprise when she opened the door. "Wow," he said. "You look…that dress is…spectacular."

"It's not the dress," Mary said. "It's the woman wearing it." She stepped forward to hug Julia. "You look like a million dollars."

More like $2,836 and odd change. But Julia wouldn't have cared had it been twice that—five times, a hundred times. Barbara had bought the absolutely perfect little black dress. Deceptively simple, the strapless, knee-length creation clung to her best features and softly draped over those that not even jogging four miles a day could return to their ten-year-gone prime. Her shoes were two-hours-max strappy heels; her only jewelry, her wedding ring and Barbara's diamond stud earrings, which she'd insisted Julia wear.

Julia stepped outside and turned to lock the door, but her hands were shaking so badly she couldn't fit the key into the slot.

"Let me," Harold said. He locked the door, tested it and handed Julia the key. She tucked it into her bra.

"Didn't want to bother with a purse," she explained. It was then she noticed a Mercedes limo in the driveway, so new it still had paper license plates. "What's this?"

"Your ride," Mary said. "We decided that this day belongs to you and Evan."

Mary must have worked her magic on Barbara, too, because when Julia invited her to ride to the airport with them, she'd declined, saying her absence was the first of an armload of gifts she had to give Evan. Julia glanced at Harold. There was no way he'd agreed to wait a whole day without heavy persuasion. She hugged him. "Thank you."

He nodded. "Tell Evan—" Overcome with emotions, he caught his lower lip between his teeth. "Tell him welcome home and that we'll see him tomorrow."

"For breakfast," Mary said. "At our house. As soon as you're up and feel like company."

Julia hugged her, long and hard. "I owe you two so much."

"Nonsense," Mary said, and then smiled. "But you do realize that 'as soon as you feel like coming over' means no later than eight. I had to promise Harold I'd do whatever it took to get you there by then."

Julia laughed. "We'll be there."

"And then if you and Evan feel up to it, we thought we'd have a little reception at the house this weekend. Somehow word got out that he's en route and it was the only way we could manage all the friends who were calling."

That would give them three days, one alone and two with Shelly and Jason. "I'll check with Evan, but I don't see why that wouldn't work."

Actually, she could think of several reasons Evan might not want to be in a crowd, even one made up of loving family and friends. The books she'd read about hostages coming home after long captivities had been filled with stories about stress and illnesses, both mental and physical. But worrying about that on the happiest day of her life was like winning the Miss America contest and stopping to make sure none of the stones in the crown were loose.

She looked from Mary to Harold to Barbara. "I couldn't have gotten through all these years without you," she told them. "Thank you." She put her hand to her chest. "From the bottom of my heart."

Tears filled Barbara's eyes. "You taught me the true meaning of love, Julia. I'll never settle for anything less again."

Julia kissed her sister and took a second to wipe the lipstick from her cheek before giving Harold and Mary quick hugs. The chauffeur got out and opened the door. Julia hurried toward the car as fast as her sexy, completely impractical heels would allow, then stopped for one last wave before disappearing behind smoked glass.

Two doors down she saw her neighbor Marjorie Wells, standing in the middle of her front yard, about to plant a sign that said Welcome Home, Evan. This was a woman who'd moved in two years ago, someone who only knew Evan through her and the kids.

Julia spotted a small jet in the distance and watched, transfixed, as it banked and circled and prepared to land. She knew without question Evan was inside. All the years of waiting had come down to minutes. Her hands tingled, a warning for her to stop holding her breath. She moved outside.

Another hangar kept her from seeing the actual landing, but she heard the jets back off and knew the plane was on the ground. Minutes later it appeared, taxiing toward her. Her heartbeat thundered in her ears, louder even than the idling jet engines. She scanned the small windows but couldn't see inside past the reflecting sun. The wind whipped her hair. The plane stopped…

*After all this time, could it really be true that Evan had come home to her?*

The door opened. Stairs appeared. A man filled the doorway. He found her, and his face lit with a brilliant smile.

"Evan," she breathed.

He was here. He was really here.

Her legs wouldn't move. Evan was home. She didn't have to be strong or rigid or carry the world on her shoulders anymore. She didn't run to him; she couldn't. Instead, her heart and mind reached for him. He crossed the tarmac and swept her into his arms.

With a cry she melted against him, her arms locked around his neck. Now, at this moment, she truly believed he was home.

She leaned back to look into his eyes. "It's really you," she said in wonder.

He was thinner and his hair had more gray, new lines framed his eyes and there was a long scar on his chin that hadn't been there before. He was wearing dark-green slacks and a plaid shirt, clothes obviously borrowed, in colors he would never have picked for himself. But he was not the emaciated, sickly man she'd feared he would be after all the years he'd spent in the jungle.

Before she could say anything more, he lowered his mouth to hers. The kiss was the one she'd dreamed of in the morning when the kids had gone to school and the house echoed in loneliness, when she looked around at a world seemingly occupied by pairs; and in the middle of the night when her mind allowed her to go to a place where she was free of the agony of missing him.

"I'm here because of you," he said, cupping her face with his hands, absorbing her with his eyes. "I knew you were waiting." He gave her a breath-stealing smile. "I couldn't disappoint you."

She was crying, unable to return his smile. "I would have waited forever."

"I know," he said softly. "I always knew."

She touched the scar on his chin. "How—"

He took her hand and pressed his lips to her palm. "It's nothing. A story for another time." He kissed her again. "I want to go home."

Julia nodded.

Loud clapping erupted around them. Julia jumped, startled. She'd forgotten they weren't alone. Evan smiled in acknowledgment of the well wishes and waved. He put his arm around Julia and leaned in close to whisper, "Where's the car?"

# CHAPTER 16

"Incredible dress," Evan said, following Julia into the limo.

An ordinary compliment filled with extraordinary meaning. "Barbara picked it out for me."

"Remind me to thank her." He settled in beside her, locking his seat belt and taking her hand. "I was expecting a crowd. How did you talk everyone out of coming?"

"We have Mary to thank for that."

His smile faded, his expression serious once more. "It's going to take a long time to thank all the people who worked to bring me home."

"There are a lot of wonderful people eager to meet you," she said.

"You must have made some important friends. I flew in first class with a State Department escort all the way from Bogotá to San Francisco. There wasn't a barrier that came up in Miami that he didn't knock down with a phone call. How did you manage to maintain these people's attention spans all this time?"

"I never went away." Was she really having this conversation? Was it really her hand clasped in his? She touched his cheek, his chin, his nose, his hair. "You're really here," she said in wonder.

"It's hard for me to believe, too."

"What do you want to do?"

He gave her a throaty laugh filled with meaning. "You mean besides the obvious?"

For the second time that day, she blushed. "Afterward. You have a list," she insisted. "I know you made one, if only in your mind."

He laughed again, this time joyfully. Could there be a sweeter sound? "I've been dreaming about a garlic-tomato-and-olive pizza," he told her.

"And?" she prodded.

"Brunch with you at Venita Rhea's. Please tell me they're still in business. I used to wake up dreaming about their olive-and-mushroom omelets."

"They're still there. No olives in the jungle?" She

caught her breath in surprise at the question. Could she be joking with him about their ordeal?

He leaned over to kiss her. "Thank you," he said, his voice cracking. "I need to be home again. I need to have things the way they were—normal."

Her heart went out to him. "I'll do what I can, but there are people who—"

"I know. I expect that. I just want to get through it as quickly as possible so we can get back to our lives." He squeezed her hand in reassurance as he looked out at a suburban landscape almost unchanged in five years. "I'm worried about reconnecting with Shelly and Jason," he reluctantly admitted. He looked back at her. "Do they even remember me?"

"Not the way I do, but you are as real to them as you are to me." There was nothing she could say to reassure him. Only being with his children again, seeing for himself how much they'd changed and how much they'd stayed the same, would give him what he needed. "They'll be here tomorrow at noon. It was the first flight Dad could get."

"I tried calling them when we landed in Miami, but Fred told me that they'd already left for Kansas City. I should have made time before I left Bogotá, but they were already holding the plane." He stared out the window again, this time seeing Sacramento's city skyline, radically different from when he'd left.

"All these new buildings. Everything has changed so much."

"Not me," she said softly.

He turned back to her and smiled. "Even you," he said. "You've grown more beautiful."

The amazing thing was that she believed him. She knew without question that in his eyes, she would still be as beautiful at eighty. She leaned over and put her head on his shoulder. "I tried to imagine what your days were like. It hurt so much to think of you being mistreated or locked away that I finally stopped."

"For the most part I suffered more monotony than abuse."

"I have so many questions I don't know where to begin. We never did find out who took you or why. Every time we thought we had it figured out, another group would make contact."

"I'm afraid that's my fault. I kept escaping but never made it very far before I was recaptured by someone else. In the beginning it was a bunch of stupid thugs who simply screwed up and snatched the wrong man. They had no idea what to do with me when the people who'd hired them refused to pay. I spent months with them traveling from village to village before I realized I was being shopped around to groups that knew how the ransom process worked.

"Finally, they just dumped me with someone's

cousin who said he knew some guys who would keep me until they found someone who would pay. These guys realized I had no sense of direction, and I became their source of entertainment. They'd take me a couple of miles from camp and leave me just to see how lost I could get.

"One day they left me near a stream. I followed it and a week later wound up in a village controlled by FARC. They were a little more savvy about controlling their captives and it took me longer to get away from them."

"How many times did you escape?"

He put his arm around her and settled her deeper into his side. "Successfully? Only once."

"And unsuccessfully?"

"A dozen times. I wound up with six different groups."

"It must have been the FARC group that sent the first note," she said. "We couldn't figure out why they waited so long to make contact."

"I probably should have stayed put," he said. "But all I could think about was getting home to you and the kids."

At last, all the ransom demands by different groups made sense. How was it that none of them had ever figured it out?

"For the most part I was with people who knew I was useless to them dead. And since no one knew how long it would take to get their money, it was in their interest to feed me and keep me as healthy as possible."

Julia slipped her arm around his waist, still struggling to comprehend that Evan was really there beside her, that it wasn't a dream. "We got reports of a tall white man with black hair and blue eyes, but every sighting was so far apart from the last one that we didn't think the reports could be trusted."

He chuckled. "Next time I'll know not to going wandering around."

Julia reared back. The olives were one thing, but how could he joke about a wound so deep it was still bleeding? "Don't say that."

He touched her cheek and then her lips with his fingertips, mapping her face. "It's over, Julia. I'm home. You can let it go now."

Did he really think that was possible? "I can't."

"I never believed it would be possible to put what happened to my mother and brother behind me, either, but you showed me I could. We have to find a way to let this go, too."

His mother and brother were his pain, something she hadn't experienced, something she could philosophize about from a safe distance. Not until now did she truly understand what she'd asked of him back then. "I don't know if I can."

He touched his forehead to hers in a gesture as

intimate as a kiss. "If you don't, you give what happened power over everything you do or say or feel for the rest of your life. Every sorrow will feel deserved and every joy will be dampened by fear. I know this, Julia, because I lived it before I met you."

"You can really forgive them for what they did?" That's what he was asking. She couldn't forget without forgiving. "This easily?"

"It's either that or let them have power over me. Why would I want to do that?"

They weren't just words. "I don't know how," she admitted. "It's been my life for almost six years. It's all I've thought about. How do I stop being angry for all the Thanksgivings and Christmases and birthdays we missed with you? And all the ordinary moments that make up memories we'll never share?"

"Look at me." She did. "You were told I was dead. You buried me. And yet I'm here with you now. Do you really want our lives forever tainted by the men who put us through that hell?"

He was telling her what she needed to hear, what she'd told him twenty years ago. How easy it had seemed in theory, how hard in execution. "If I could, I would castrate every last one of them."

Evan laughed, deep and hearty. "That's my Julia."

"But since I can't," she added, "I'll find a way to forget them."

# CHAPTER 17

Evan stood at the open sliding-glass door with Julia at his side and stared at the backyard, awash in a brilliant orange sunset. "It's exactly the way I imagined. Even more beautiful. You did an incredible job."

"Shelly helped." She smiled. "And the gardener I hired when I was doing so much traveling."

He put his arm around her shoulders and drew her into his side. "Tell me about the dog."

Pearl was busy investigating this new territory, an investigation Julia had cut short when she'd left for the airport. She'd been afraid that if she left Pearl outside, she would spook and escape through one of the weak spots in the twenty-year-old wooden fence.

Julia also worried what Pearl would do when yet another man invaded her territory, especially one who wouldn't yield to her threats. But instead of the fierce greeting she'd given Harold, Pearl stood her ground and stared at Evan for a full minute before going to the door and scratching to be let out.

Julia told him about Pearl and David and how meeting them had saved her sanity that summer.

"Do you think he'll stop by if he makes it this far?" Evan asked.

Julia shook her head. "He fell a little in love with me. When he realized I could never reciprocate his feelings, he left."

Evan didn't say anything for a long time. "You thought I was dead. I would understand if you—"

"It didn't matter that I believed I would never see you again, Evan. If I'd never known your love… I could have found someone else. But almost losing you made me understand what it means to have connected to my soul mate. This is for life. Nothing can change that."

He kissed her. She came up on her toes to return the kiss, to feel the length of his body against hers. A long-banked fire exploded in her. Tentacles of flame turned gentle passion into raging need.

Evan ran his hands down her back and over the soft rise of her buttocks. He cupped the flesh and brought her closer, his desire hard and throbbing.

She clasped his hand and led him upstairs to their room, to the bed where they'd made sweet, familiar love the last night they'd had together. He sat her on the corner of the mattress and lifted one foot and then the other, removing her heels and kissing the arch of each foot. She reached for her zipper and he caught her hand. "Let me."

"Hurry," she urged.

He did, but stopped to look at her when she lay naked across the bed. "I remember a hay field and a girl I thought the most perfect ever created. That was nothing compared with what you are now."

She undid the buttons on his shirt. Her fingers shook in fevered anticipation and she fumbled getting them undone. Impatient, Evan grabbed the hem and pulled the shirt over his head.

Julia gasped when she saw his chest and arms. He was covered in scars, some so fresh that they were still red. "What—"

He placed a hand over her mouth to silence her. "Another time, Julia. Not now."

He'd lied to her. His life hadn't been lived in the benign captivity he'd implied. How could he ask her to forgive the men who had done this to him? She pressed her palm against his chest, feeling his heart, the heart that had survived untold horrors to bring him back to her.

He had survived for her.

He had lived through a hell she could only imagine to return home to her, even when it would have been easier to stop trying. The depth of his love was more than she could comprehend. "Thank you for not giving up," she said through her tears. "Without you I would have been alone forever."

"Don't cry," he said softly. "I came home. I'm here. Nothing else matters."

She placed her arms around his neck and kissed him, tasting his lips and her tears, surrendering herself to his desire to forget. She ran her fingers over his scars, making them something she shared with him, erasing their power and thoughts of the men who had put them there. He stood and removed the rest of his clothes and she saw there were more scars, so many that there were few places on his body left untouched.

Julia sat up. "Turn around."

He did, exposing his brutalized back.

She tried, but couldn't stop the tears. "I've always believed that seventeen-year-old boy I made love to on my grandmother's patchwork quilt was the standard I would use to judge every other man against. I've changed my mind."

Evan turned to her and smiled. "Why, Mrs. Prescott, I believe that's the sexiest thing anyone has ever said to me."

"Come here," she told him, holding out her

arms. "If you think that was sexy, wait until you see what I have—"

Evan covered her mouth with his, and the rest of what she was going to say was lost forever.

Julia awoke with a start. Evan was gone. For one heartbreaking moment she was almost overwhelmed by a terrible fear that he'd never been there at all, that she'd been dreaming he was home, dreaming that he'd made love to her, dreaming that he'd told her he loved her over and over again until her heart was ready to burst with joy. But then she saw his clothes draped over the chair in the corner and she could breathe again.

She swung her legs over the side of the bed to go look for Evan and almost stepped on him. He was sleeping on the rug she kept beside the bed, dressed in his old pajama bottoms, holding something white. Julia crawled out the other side of the bed and came around to look at him.

The "white" tucked into his arms was Pearl. She raised her head just enough to acknowledge Julia, thumped her tail twice and let out a contented sigh before settling back down, her nose resting on Evan's arm.

Two lost souls had recognized each other. Almost as if it had been predestined—if Julia believed in such things.

She backtracked to get her robe. Placing her hand on the nightstand for balance, she stepped into her slippers and accidentally bumped Evan's rose. A petal dropped, and then another. Slowly the rose shed its petals one after the other until they lay in a perfect circle around the vase. It was as if Evan's homecoming had released the rose from its burden.

Julia stood and stared, transfixed. "Okay, Mother," she whispered. "I give up. You were right."

She gathered the petals and slipped them in her pocket to take downstairs and put in the wooden box David had given her, saving them to pass on to Shelly and Jason one day, maybe at their weddings, or maybe when they became parents. Her mother would like that.

In the meantime, she had a letter to finish.

Dante Raintree stood with his arms crossed as he watched the woman on the monitor. The image was in black and white to better show details; color distracted the brain. He focused on her hands, watching every move she made, but what struck him most was how uncommonly *still* she was. She didn't fidget or play with her chips, or look around at the other players. She peeked once at her down card, then didn't touch it again, signaling for another hit by tapping a fingernail on the table. Just because she didn't seem to be paying attention to the other players, though, didn't mean she was as unaware as she seemed.

"What's her name?" Dante asked.

"Lorna Clay," replied his chief of security, Al Rayburn.

"At first I thought she was counting, but she doesn't pay enough attention."

"She's paying attention, all right," Dante murmured. "You just don't see her doing it." A card counter had to remember every card played. Supposedly counting cards was impossible with the number of decks used by the casinos, but there were those rare individuals who could calculate the odds even with multiple decks.

"I thought that, too," said Al. "But look at this piece of tape coming up. Someone she knows comes up to her and speaks, she looks around and starts chatting, completely misses the play of the people to her left—and doesn't look around even when the deal comes back to her, just taps that finger. And damn if she didn't win. Again."

Dante watched the tape, rewound it, watched it again. Then he watched it a third time. There had to be something he was missing, because he couldn't pick out a single giveaway.

"If she's cheating," Al said with something like respect, "she's the best I've ever seen."

"What does your gut say?"

Al scratched the side of his jaw, considering. Finally, he said, "If she isn't cheating, she's the luckiest person walking. She wins. Week in, week out, she wins. Never a huge amount, but I ran the numbers and she's into us for about five grand a week. Hell, boss, on her way out of the casino she'll stop by a slot machine, feed a dollar in and walk away with at least fifty. It's never the same machine, either. I've had her watched, I've had her followed, I've even looked for the same faces in the casino every time she's in here, and I can't find a common denominator."

"Is she here now?"

"She came in about half an hour ago. She's playing blackjack, as usual."

"Bring her to my office," Dante said, making a swift decision. "Don't make a scene."

"Got it," said Al, turning on his heel and leaving the security center.

Dante left, too, going up to his office. His face was calm. Normally he would leave it to Al to deal with a cheater, but he was curious. How was she doing it? There were a lot of bad cheaters, a few good ones, and every so often one would come along who was the stuff of which legends were made: the cheater who didn't get caught, even when people were alert and the camera was on him—or, in this case, her.

It was possible to simply be lucky, as most people understood luck. Chance could turn a habitual loser into a big-time winner. Casinos, in fact, thrived on that hope. But luck itself wasn't habitual, and he knew that what passed for luck was often something else: cheating. And there was the other kind of luck, the kind he himself possessed, but it depended not on chance but on who and what he was. He knew it was an innate power and not Dame Fortune's erratic smile. Since power like his was rare, the odds made it likely the woman he'd been watching was merely a very clever cheat.

Her skill could provide her with a very good living, he thought, doing some swift calculations in his head. Five grand a week equaled $260,000 a year, and that was just from his casino. She probably hit them all, careful to keep the numbers relatively low so she stayed under the radar.

He wondered how long she'd been taking him, how long she'd been winning a little here, a little there, before Al noticed.

The curtains were open on the wall-to-wall window in his office, giving the impression, when one first opened the door, of stepping out onto a covered balcony. The glazed window faced west, so he could catch the sunsets. The sun was low now, the sky painted in purple and gold. At his home in the mountains, most of the windows faced east, affording him views of the sunrise. Something in him needed both the greeting and the goodbye of the sun. He'd always been drawn to sunlight, maybe because fire was his element to call, to control.

He checked his internal time: four minutes until sundown. Without checking the sunrise tables every day, he knew exactly when the sun would slide behind the mountains. He didn't own an alarm clock. He didn't need one. He was so acutely attuned to the sun's position that he had only to check within himself to know the time. As for waking at a particular time, he was one of those people who could tell himself to wake at a certain time, and he did. That talent had nothing to do with being Raintree, so he didn't have to hide it; a lot of perfectly ordinary people had the same ability.

He had other talents and abilities, however, that did require careful shielding. The long days of summer instilled in him an almost sexual high, when he could feel contained power buzzing just beneath his skin. He had to be doubly careful not to cause candles to leap into flame just by his presence, or to start wildfires with a glance in the dry-as-tinder brush. He loved Reno; he didn't want to burn it down. He just felt so damn *alive* with all the sunshine pouring down that he wanted to let the energy pour through him instead of holding it inside.

This must be how his brother Gideon felt while pulling lightning, all that hot power searing through his muscles, his veins. They had this in common, the connection with raw power. All the members of the far-flung Raintree clan had some power, some heightened ability, but only members of the royal family could channel and control the earth's natural energies.

Dante wasn't just of the royal family, he was the Dranir, the leader of the entire clan. "Dranir" was synonymous with king, but the position he held wasn't ceremonial, it was one of sheer power. He was the oldest son of the previous Dranir, but he would have been passed over for the position if he hadn't also inherited the power to hold it.

Behind him came Al's distinctive knock on the door. The outer office was empty, Dante's secretary having gone home hours before. "Come in," he called, not turning from his view of the sunset.

The door opened, and Al said, "Mr. Raintree, this is Lorna Clay."

Dante turned and looked at the woman, all his senses on alert. The first thing he noticed was the vibrant color of her hair, a rich, dark red that encompassed a multitude of shades from copper to burgundy. The warm amber light danced along the iridescent strands, and he felt a hard tug of sheer lust in his gut. Looking at her hair was almost like looking at fire, and he had the same reaction.

The second thing he noticed was that she was spitting mad.

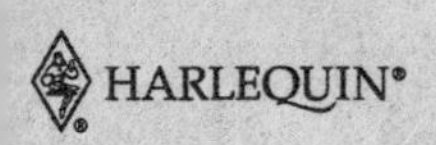
HARLEQUIN®

Silhouette

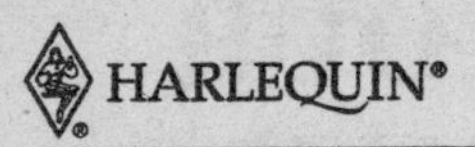
HARLEQUIN®
American ROMANCE®

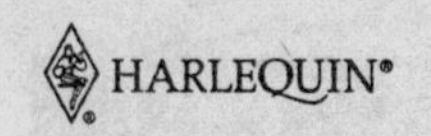

EVERLASTING LOVE™

*Every great love has a story to tell™*

# COMING NEXT MONTH

**#7. *The Marriage Bed* by Judith Arnold**

The marriage bed—the one place above all where a husband and wife can be honest with each other. But after an old boyfriend of Joelle DiFranco's suddenly reappears and she hears his anguished plea, Joelle and Bobby, her husband of thirty-seven years, are forced to rethink the entire premise of their marriage....

**#8. *Family Stories* by Tessa McDermid**

When Frank and Marian meet in 1929, they realize they're destined to spend the rest of their lives together. In the face of disapproval from Marian's parents, they elope, determined to start their marriage, and discover that *wanting* a life together and *making* one are two different things. But through it all, they share a love that affects everyone in their family—from then until now.

www.eHarlequin.com

HECNM0407